JUNGLE RABHA MASKS AND MASKED DANCE

JUNGLE RABHA MASKS AND MASKED DANCE
An Antropological Documentation

Sabita Ranjan Sarkar

Indira Gandhi Rashtriya Manav Sangrahalaya
(National Museum of Mankind Bhopal)

GYAN

ISBN : 978-81-2121-306-6
Price : ₹ 650/-

First Published 2015

Published by

Gyan Publishing House
5, Ansari Road,
Daryaganj, New Delhi-110002
Mob: 9811692060
E-Mail:books@gyanbooks.com
Website: www.gyanbooks.com

and

Indira Gandhi Rashtriya Manav Sangrahalaya
Shamla Hills, Bhopal
Phones: 0755-2661290, 2661319
Fax: 91-755-2661458

Printed at : G. Print Process, Delhi

Cataloging in Publication Data—DK
Courtesy: D.K. Agencies (P) Ltd. <docinfo@dkagencies.com>

Sarkar, Sabita Ranjan, 1934- **author.**
Jungle Rabha masks and masked dance : an anthropological documentation / Sabita Ranjan Sarkar.
pages cm
Includes bibliographical references.
ISBN 9788121213066

1. Rabha (Indic people)—Social life and customs. 2. Rabha (Indic people)—Clothing—India—Jalpaiguri (District) 3. Rabha (Indic people)—Clothing—India—Koch Bihar (District) 4. Dance—Anthropological aspects—India—Jalpaiguri (District) 5. Dance—anthropological aspects—India—Koch Bihar (District) 6. Folk dancing—India—Jalpaiguri (District) 7. Folk dancing—India—Koch Bihar (District) I. Title.

DS432.R2S27 2015 DDC 305.80095414 23

Contents

Fig. 1: A View of the *Sal* Forest of Western Duars

Foreword

This book is a valuable outcome of fieldwork initiative taken more than three decades back by the author as a member of the anthropology section of the Indian museum. This book has multiple implications to understand one of the fundamental essences of anthropological discourse embedded within the idea of 'Holism' leading to the understanding of the mask dance (Char-Khilanee) in an ethnographic perspective. It reveals how a tradition can be evolved in the process of negotiation with the wider sociological context. It underscores the strength of empiricism for understanding even a object like mask which has a distinct place in understanding inter-community as well as intra- community relations within a specific ecological niche and may also reflect ideological space for rethinking the notion of 'Saced –Secular Continuum ' taking example of Rabhas located in Charduars within a multi-ethnic setting.

Author deserves huge appreciation for revealing how material culture can metaphorically lead us to explore larger socio-political processes to understand the resultant change occurred in tribal social formations living in close contact with the Hindu societies. I am sure this book will inspire many other museum personnel and curators with anthropological bend of mind to develop similar initiatives out of their own institutional collections or taking further initiatives through field research as it is generally agreed upon that in the ultimate contextual analysis any museum object must tell us the larger multilayered tales of existential reality. IGRMS always tried to promote such valuable publication so that it can be accessed by wider readers/scholars who care such issues linked with tribal population of India

Prof. Sarit Kumar Chaudhuri
Director
Indira Gandhi Rashtriya Manav Sangrahalaya
Shamla Hills, Bhopal(MP)

Acknowledgements

This is the revised version of an anthropological field report which is the partial output of an extensive field work undertaken by the author among the Jungle Rabhas – a tribal group of North Bengal. He sought the help of several scholars and technicians to prepare this report for publication. As such, the author owes a debt to each one of them.

To begin with, the author owes a special debt of gratitude to Jungle Rabhas, the inhabitants of Pore Bastee who extended full co-operation during the field work in the region. First and foremost among the individuals who deserve special thanks from the author is Dr S. Roy who offered him opportunity to undertake this field work and also constantly and enthusiastically encouraged him to keep it up.

The author takes this opportunity to offer his sincere thanks to Benu Sen and D. Gayen, the Photographers who took much pain in taking the photographs in the field situation and also for taking all the troubles to make them prepared for this publication. The author extends heartfelt thanks to Smt Kusumita Bhattacharya, an artist who prepared all the sketches meant for the publication.

The author would like to express his thanks to Dr R.K. Bhattacharya, former Director of the

Anthropological Survey of India for going through the script. The author particularly owes a debt to Dr Satyabrata Chakraborty, former Deputy Director, Anthropological Survey of India. He meticulously went through the script and offered valuable suggestions to improve upon it from anthropological standpoint.

Last of all the author offers his deep gratitude to Prof. Sarit Kumar Choudhury, Director, Indira Gandhi Rashtriya Manav Sangrahalaya who helped in a multitude of ways to bring this work to fruition. Without his active effort it would take more time to bring it out in published form.

Sabita Ranjan Sarkar

Preface

The author as a museum-based anthropologist started anthropological field work for the first time in North Bengal among the Rabhas, one of the scheduled tribes of Jalpaiguri and Coochbehar districts. The field work was undertaken in the early part of 1980s. There are two sections of the Rabhas—Village Rabhas and Jungle Rabhas. Contrary to the Village Rabhas, the Jungle Rabhas are still living in the jungle belt mostly as forest labourers. Even now they possess many of their traditional culture traits. Under the process of acculturation, many of their traditional cultural elements are at present under constant threat of extinction. It is, therefore, high time for the collection of the relics of traditional Rabha culture before they sink into oblivion. So the author selected the Jungle Rabhas of district Jalpaiguri for the collection of their traditional cultural artifacts and also to study the cultural history of some of the important items of their material culture. One of the most significant items in the Rabha collection is their masks which have now become obsolete as the masked dance is no longer practised.

Collection is the backbone of a museum. As such, one of the basic functions of the anthropological museums is to collect the traditional cultural artifacts from time to time to enrich their collection. These collections are meant not only to preserve them for the posterity and to organise their display in the gallery for imparting visual education to the visiting public but also for carrying out their study and research from anthropological standpoint. Such study may provide adequate data for understanding the trend of traditional culture offering scope for reconstruction of regional cultural history. To discharge this responsibility the author took up the study of *Char-Khilainee*, a masked dance of the Jungle Rabhas. The data of this dance which author collected during the field trips in 1982 and 1983, have been utilised in this publication to record the culture and history of the dance. The data of the dance collected in 1982 and 1983 are concerned with its past account. In view of its past record, the data collected in early 1980s are still relevant in 2015. It is through this publication, an attempt has been made to keep on record an account of the masked dance of the Jungle Rabhas for the posterity.

During the pre-British period the Jungle Rabhas used to live in the deep interior of the forest. They practised shifting cultivation and hunting-gathering economy. With no communication facilities they kept themselves strictly confined to the jungle areas. As such, they had no connection with the external world. Natural hazards, unhygienic condition, political instability, lack of communication facilities stood in the way of attracting outsiders to this dissolute place. Forest oriented physical environment, traditional simple technology and typical subsistence pattern of the jungle dwelling Rabhas played the vital role in determining their traditional culture pattern.

Like any other tribal community, dance and music are the integral parts of the cultural life of the Jungle

Rabhas. But the masked dance (*Char-Khilainee*) was not associated with their traditional cultural life. Concept of mask and masked dance was introduced at a later stage when the scope of acculturation among them was considerably increased. However, this masked dance among the Jungle Rabhas did not last long. Within a short span of time the dance made its exit from their cultural life primarily due to change in both physical and cultural environment, followed by the change in tribal economy, government forest policy and others. Taking *Char-Khilainee* dance as an example of cultural event, it has been examined here to what extent habitat, ecology, economy and technology have played positive role not only in introducing but also in discarding this performing art from the life of the Jungle Rabhas.

The study deals with different factors like physical environment of western Duars, distribution pattern of the regional tribes, their traditional technology, change in their subsistence pattern, extent of acculturation among them and change in government forest policy from time to time. These factors are believed to be responsible for the origin, development, perpetuation and extinction of this masked dance. To bring out a clear picture in different stages of its existence, the historiography of the dance has been divided into three phases - pre-British, British and post-British. Here attempt has been made here to ascertain the status of the dance in each phase for bringing out a clear picture as to how physical environment, government forest policy, acculturation and economic activities in particular, had exerted their influence on the rise and fall of this performing art.

In making the collection special emphasis was given on those cultural artifacts which had relative importance in the cultural life, but had either become extinct or were on the verge of extinction by then. Holistic study was made on them to keep in record of all the related information available right from their origin, touching upon propagation, functional role, structural features, technological aspect and the causes of extinction. As the vestigial relics of traditional culture, the study on masks of the Jungle Rabhas and the associated masked dance (*Char-Khilainee*) was included in this project.

Field work among the Jungle Rabhas of district Jalpaiguri was taken up for making ethnographic collection during 1982 and 1983. By that time, the masked dance under study was no longer in practice. Related masks were also not prepared. Full-fledged *Char-Khilainee* dance was found in its true colour only upto the early part of 1950s. But some of the elderly people who could prepare the masks and once participated in the dance were still there in 1980s. The author, leader of the field party took advantage of the situation. He got the masks used in *Char-Khilainee* dance prepared by the competent mask-makers who were then still alive. The field data associated with the related masks were also collected from the elderly Rabhas who once organised and participated in the dance. The field documentation work done on the masks of *Char-Khilainee* dance was holistic. It covered the collection of masks along with anthropological field data associated with them together with photographic documentation both in still and video, depicting their structural features, manufacturing technology and functional role. Costumes and choreography of the dance were also pictorially documented. Those field data collected during this field work and photographs taken on the occasion, have been incorporated in this publication for keeping on record the information of *Char-Khilanee*, an obsolete masked dance which once played an important role in the social life of the Jungle Rabhas and made significant contribution in certain spheres of their cultural life.

Kolkata
2015

Sabita Ranjan Sarkar

List of Figures

1

Introduction

I

Music

Music is an art of organising or controlling sounds for maintaining tune, rhythm and musical concord, not merely in a way that is technically correct but in a manner that satisfies the human sense. As a technical term it implies the observance of some kind of measures which are particularly applied to dancing and singing. Hence music is used as a blanket term which includes both these categories of performing art.

Music and human culture

Music is an important aspect of human culture. It is universal. Music is found at all levels of culture from the most primitive rural folk to the high technologically advanced and sophisticated urban people. It had its origin in prehistoric past when mankind was in his infancy. Since then it has been continuing till now in full glory without loosing its grace and functional potentiality at any point of time. Since the emergence of man as culture bearing animal, music is integrally associated with human culture. Geographically music is also traced all over the world to all ecological settings. Multifarious functional roles which music has been playing in cultural life through the ages is made it widespread and deep-rooted in human culture.

Functional role of music

Functionally music plays an important role in the cultural life of man covering different aspects. It is one of the best channels of communication of human sentiment. Both pathos and joy are expressed through music. It relieves man from tension, fatigue and monotony. It inspires man for the noble cause, arouses patriotic sentiment, strengthens group solidarity and communicates a message. As a channel of communication, it propagates history and traditions of human culture. It is one of the best media for deriving pleasure both individually and collectively. Both musicians and the audience simultaneously derive pleasure through music. The Rhythmic sound of music on the one hand inspires the working spirit of the labourers and on the other lulls the kiddies. Social ceremonies and religious festivals are very often marked by music either for recreation or as the medium of communication for invoking the spiritual world. Thus considering its various functional aspects it is found that music not only plays positive role in social life but also makes substantial contribution in performing magico-religious rites. Music is therefore, integrally associated with both the secular and the sacred aspects of life. Due to its multifarious functional role music is found at all cultural levels.

Music in tribal world

From time immemorial the tribal communities had been living in isolation till they came in contact with other communities. The tribes in their isolated cultural life had to remain preoccupied with their subsistence activities. In their struggle for existence with the midst of wild nature, they became exhausted and felt bore by undertaking monotonous and laborious economic activities in day to day life. To come out of boredom in life they had to take resort to recreational activities. The recreational activities are, therefore, by far one of the most essential cultural elements in tribal life. In their isolated cultural life there was no scope of deriving any kind of recreation from the external sources. Therefore, the tribal folk had to arrange for their recreational activities by themselves in their own ways of synchronising with the physical and cultural environments. The recreational activities are by far the best media of deriving enjoyment. Enjoyment on its part removes the agony of life bringing in a fresh lease of life. There are different kinds of recreational activities in the tribal world for deriving enjoyment of which music is by far the most common. Irrespective of age and sex it is widely practised in different spheres of cultural life.

Music is one of the inherent qualities of man. It is spontaneously generated out of poetic impulse which lies dormant in one's own mind. It is not exception even among the most primitive tribes who might have lived in seclusion in the inaccessible part of the world. Outburst of human sentiment finds expression through music. This was in practice right from the prehistoric period and it holds good even today. The tribes at all levels of culture whether secluded or not have, therefore, taken up music as the channel of recreation to derive enjoyment out of it.

Having no contact with the outside world the tribes living in the isolated pockets introduced their musical tradition exclusively by themselves. Nature inspired their inherent artistic quality to find expression. The tribal musicians used to give definite tunes to their vocal music and specific rhythmic steppings to dance by following the natural surroundings of which the sounds of nature and the movement of animals were by far the most conspicuous. Singing of birds, murmuring sounds of waterways, sweet sound of leaves generated by the gentle breeze, movement of the animals, scenic beauty of the region and seasonal speciality of nature inspired the people of simple technology to give definite expression of their artistic sentiments through dance and music. As such each tribal community has so far introduced specific tunes and rhythmic steppings to their music and dance in their own characteristic style. It was of no exception in case of the more or less isolated forest dwelling Rabhas of Western Duars.

Rabha dance and music

The Rabha, a tribe living in the forest belt of Western Duars in the district Jalpaiguri of West Bengal, practically had very scanty contact with the outside world during the pre-British period. Forming small groups, each one with a very limited number of families, they lived scatteredly in the forest. Each group used to live more or less secluded life in the jungle environment and depended entirely on nature. The forest dwelling Rabhas had, therefore, no scope of acculturation during the pre-British period. Their recreation only confined to dance and music which were the outcome of their own emotion, sentiment and poetic impulse. Natural environment of Western Duars had also definite influence in attributing tunes and rhythms to their songs and dances. The dance and music were primarily the main source of recreation of the forest dwelling Rabhas. These performing arts were, therefore, ultimately associated with the different spheres of their cultural life with special reference to economic, recreational and socio-religious activities.

With no scope of acculturation, the Rabhas introduced their dance and music from the experience of their own life. For this purpose, the themes of their dance and music mostly centred around their economic activities. There were specific types of dance which they performed on the occasion of the preparation of jhum field, sowing of seeds, weeding and harvesting. Fishing technique was also depicted in dance by the Rabha females. Life in Western Duars was in constant danger in the forest belt. The forest dwelling Rabhas sought the supernatural help for their protection in the hostile environment. They liberally performed dance and music in socio-religious functions both for appeasing the deity and also for deriving enjoyment on the festive occasions and day-to-day life. The Rabhas have a few musical instruments to give proper support to their dance performance and musical recital. Nature controlled to a great extent the musical rendition of the Rabhas in the forest environment. Being mostly outdoor, under unfavourable weather condition the musical performance was avoided. Scope of organising these performing arts was very much limited when there was scarcity of food. Under favourable weather condition when the stock of paddy at home was adequate and workload in agricultural front and *Sal* (*Shorea robusta*) plantation field was bare minimum, the Rabhas used to indulge in more musical performance. Autumn, in particular, followed by winter were the ideal seasons for the purpose.

The Rabhas had special liking for dance and music. They used to participate in these performing arts outside their scheduled working hours. Ideal time was the late afternoon and the evening hours. There was scope for organising the performances both for shorter and longer duration. Both the sexes mostly in group used to participate in dance and music. Some dances were performed on the basis of gender. They could also express their sentiment through these media. The Rabha musicians and dancers introduced melody and rhythm for the dance performance and musical recital as the product of their musical impulse not only for their own satisfaction but also to satisfy the fellow Rabha villagers. The musical performances were so much dear to the Rabhas that they not only utilised them for their own enjoyment but also used them for appeasing the gods and goddesses. As such, dance and music were part and parcel of the Rabha cultural life. The Rabhas of Western Duars had so long lived in the forest belt and kept themselves isolated from the external world. Their dance and music did not get any chance to adopt any external element. Their simple performing arts were innovated exclusively by themselves.

The condition was changed with the introduction of the colonial rule in the region. Forests were declared reserved. Traditional tribal economy was very much disturbed. Cultural life was thereby affected to a great extent. Outsiders were brought into introduce new economy. Scope of acculturation was opened. Its impact could be traced in cultural life. So long the Rabhas of the jungle belt did not use any mask during the pre-British period. They introduced mask in their dance only when they came under the colonial administration. It was undoubtedly an impact of acculturation. With the change of their socio-economic condition the Rabhas started using mask as an adaptive mechanism in their cultural life. They borrowed the conception of mask from the neighbouring communities. Forest policy of the government forced the Rabhas to adopt new economic pattern. The new economic pattern exerted its influence on their social life. The mask and the masked dance introduced among the Rabhas were not only meant for recreation but also for dealing with the social problems arising out of the changed socio-economic condition. This newly introduced masked dance in the forest belt of Western Duars was in practice throughout the British rule as the new tribal economy introduced by the colonial administration remained steady during this period.

The masked dance in the forest belt of Western Duars declined sharply within a decade after independence. The Government of India introduced new forest policy for independent India at the earliest opportunity. It made some impact on the socio-economic life of the forest dwelling Rabhas. Simultaneously physical environment of Duars started undergoing considerable change. Deforestation was rampant. Population density was on the rise. Scope of acculturation was increased. Communication facilities were enhanced. Social problems which prompted the forest dwelling Rabhas to take up masked dance started declining. The regional tribal economy of the British period offered the forest dwelling Rabhas adequate scope for taking up masked dance. But this tribal economy of the British period started changing rapidly immediately after independence. Due to change in all fronts, with special reference to physical and cultural environment, tribal economy, government forest policy and many more, the masked dance which had been introduced during the British period among the forest dwelling Rabhas, as a result of acculturation, lost its ground in the new situation after independence.

Char-Khilainee was the masked dance of the forest dwelling Rabhas, a tribe living in the forest areas of Western Duars in the district Jalpaiguri of West Bengal. It was a socio-religious performing arts. Physical environment, distribution pattern of the regional tribes, change in their subsistence pattern, extent of acculturation, change in government forest policy from time to time were primarily responsible for origin, development, perpetuation and extinction of this masked dance. To bring out a clear picture in different stages of its existence, the historiography of the dance

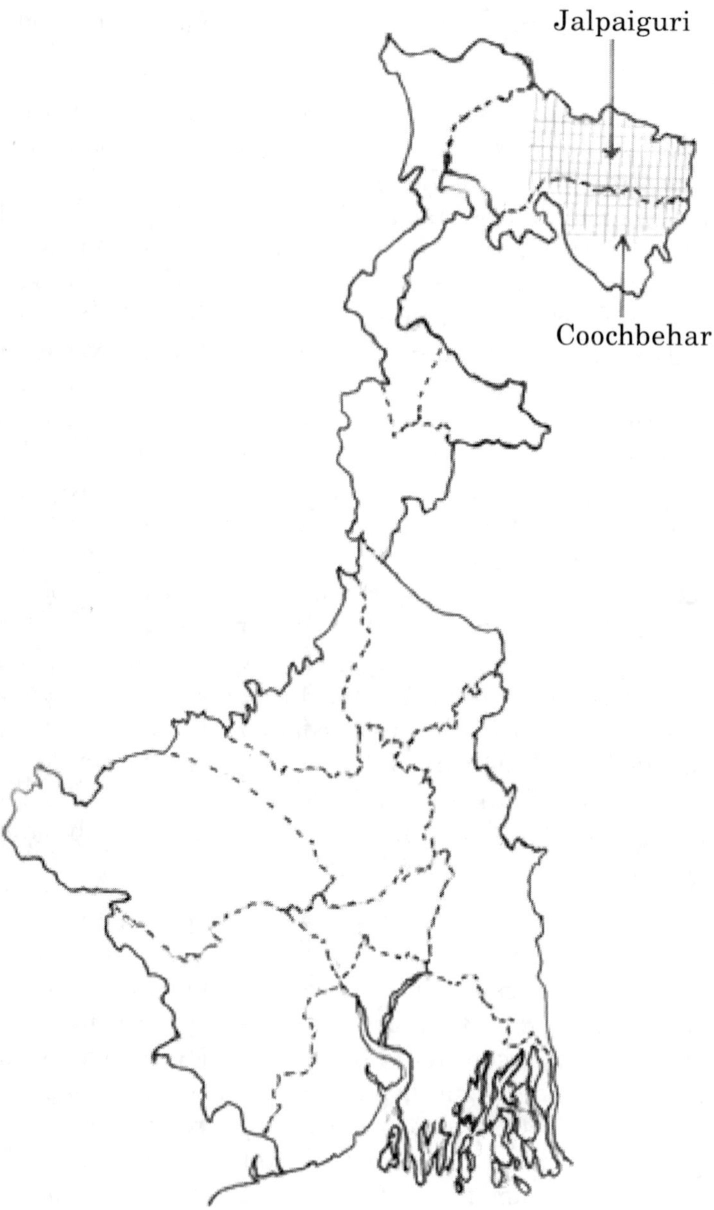

Fig. 2 : Rabha distribution in West Bengal

has been divided into three periods — pre-British, British and post-British highlighting the changing pattern of physical environment of Western Duars, government forest policy, tribal economy and acculturation. To trace out the culture history of this masked dance an attempt has been made to ascertain the status of the dance in each period for bringing out a clear picture as to how physical environment, forest policy, acculturation and economic activities in particular had exerted their respective influence on this performing art.

II
Identity of the Rabhas

The Rabhas are a little known scheduled tribe of West Bengal. Main concentration of this tribe is in Assam, the neighbouring state. They belong to the Mongoloid racial stock. In their physical characters they have similarity with the other tribes of Assam such as the Garo, Kacharis, Mech, Koch, Hajong and others who constitute the Bodo group.

Not only in physical features, but also linguistically the Rabhas have similarity with the communities belonging to the Bodo group. According to Grierson, Rabha dialect is one of the constituent elements of the Bodo languages. Pereira noticed its striking resemblance with the Atong dialect of Garo language. Endle has observed that Rabha language forms a link between Garo and Kachari. It is believed that the Rabhas are one of the constituent members of the Bodo group of Assam both from the ethnological and the linguistic point of view.

Distribution of Rabha population

The Rabhas are found only in Assam and West Bengal, two adjacent states of Eastern India. Main concentration of the Rabhas (95 per cent) is in Assam.

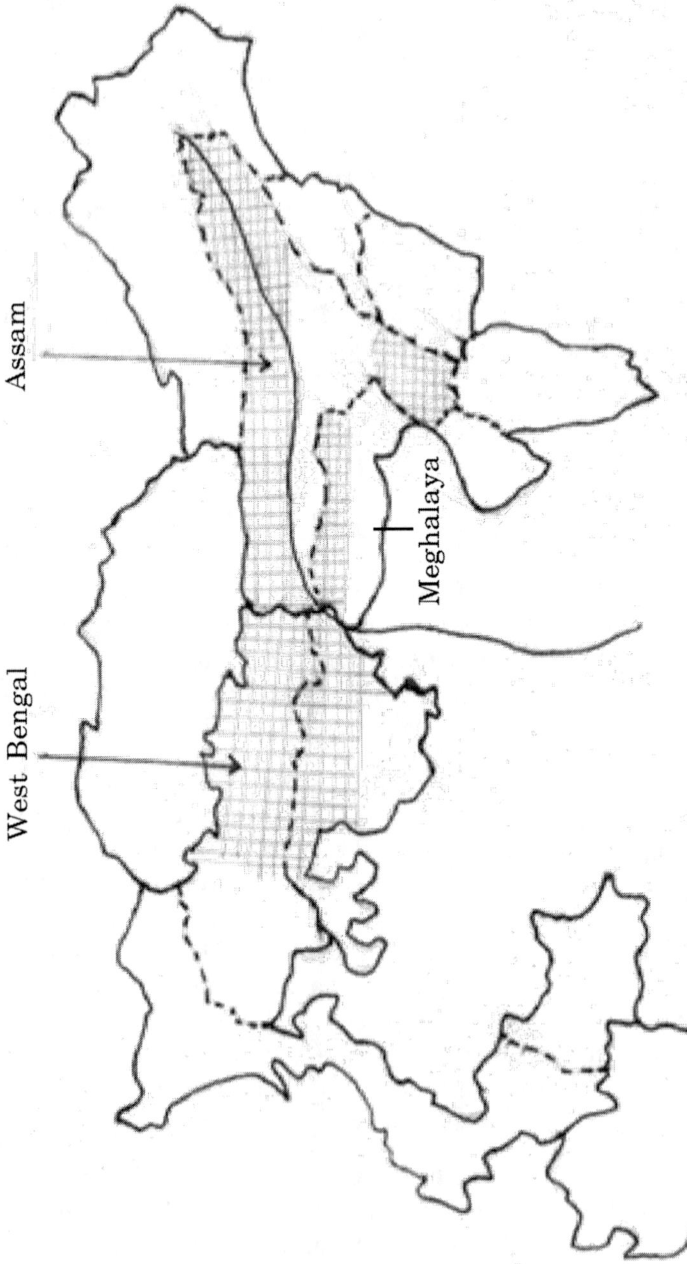

Fig. 3 : Rabha distribution in West Bengal, Assam and Meghalaya

Only 5 per cent of them live in West Bengal. Again in West Bengal, they are distributed only in two districts - Jalpaiguri (67 per cent) and Cooch Behar (13 per cent). Majority of the Rabhas (90 per cent) live particularly in the Alipurduar sub-division of district Jalpaiguri. Rabha distribution are in West Bengal, Assam and Meghalaya.

The Rabhas living in the Alipurduar sub-division are again mainly concentrated in Buxa Forest Division for its geographical location and economic opportunities.

The Alipurduar sub-division of the district Jalpaiguri belongs to Western Duars. It was land of the virgin forest when the Rabhas took shelter in this region immediately after their immigration in distant past. Jalpaiguri district is the epicentre of tribal settlement in North Bengal. Due to its geographical location and scope of enjoying the unobstructed freedom in socio-economic life, the forest belt of Western Duars was considered as heaven to the neighbouring tribes. As a result, from time immemorial different tribal groups from different regions, especially from Tibet, Nepal, Bhutan and Assam, had visited the area and settled down here making it almost exclusively a tribal zone. Again from time to time, many of these groups living in the Duars belt had left the region to seek fortune elsewhere either according to their own volition or under pressure from different quarters. New groups subsequently replaced them. The Rabhas of North Bengal are one of such immigrant groups from Assam.

Rabha migration

The history of migration of the Rabhas reveals that a section of the tribe left Assam, their home-land long back to find out suitable place for habitation elsewhere. For this purpose they started migratory movement towards the west. They passed through the Goalpara

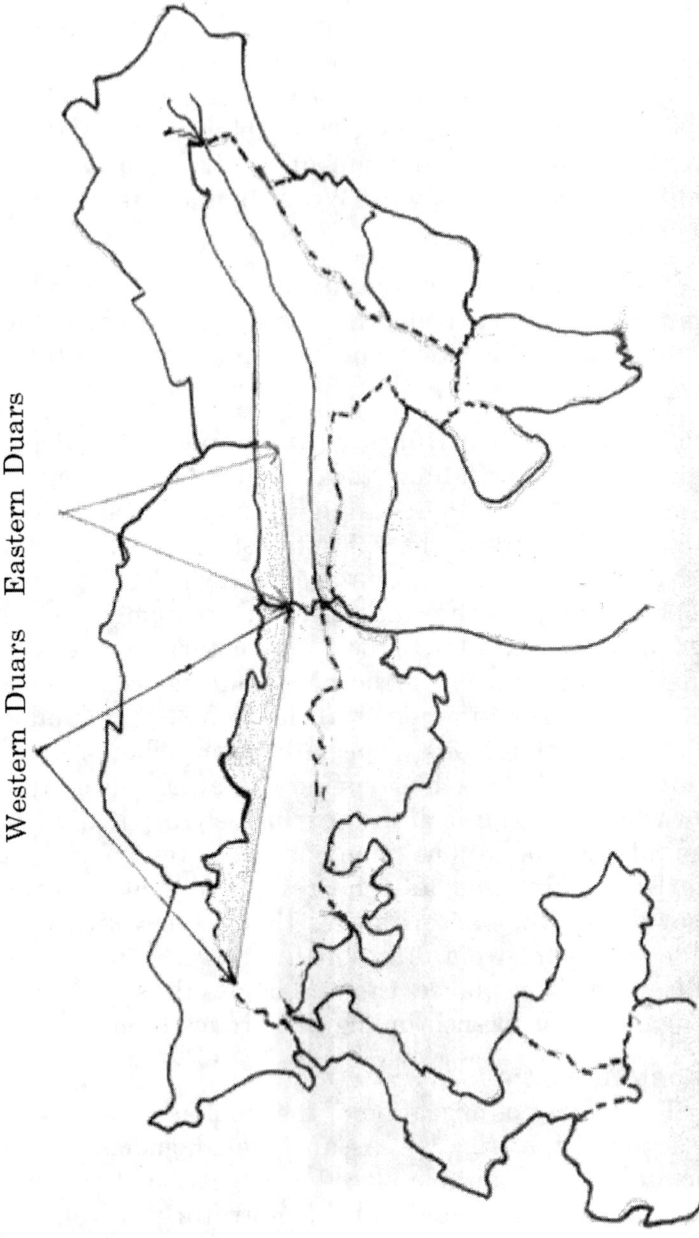

Fig. 4 : Location of Western Duars and Eastern Duars

Fig. 5 : Portrait of an oetoogenarian Rabha male

district of Assam Weastern Duars Eastern Duars along the Eastern Duars and entered the adjacent Jalpaiguri district of West Bengal. Majority of them settled down in the forest areas of Western Duars of this district, specially in the Buxa Forest Division. Throughout their journey they never deviated from their route through Duars. They selected the forest areas of Western Duars for habitation as the region was then very thinly populated with abundant supply of forest-based natural resources. They could, therefore, exploit the regional forest products and utilise forest land for subsistence activities (Rabha Migratory Route from Assam to West Bengal) without any hindrance from any quarter.

The ecological condition of the region was so ideal for practising their age-old slash and burn cultivation that they could smoothly lead their traditional cultural life.

Regional factors influencing the tribal cultures

During the pre-British period Western Duars was almost exclusively a jungle belt, sparsely populated too, mostly by the tribes. The region was most unhygienic and cut off from the outside world. The wild nature of the region had made both direct and indirect influence on the cultural life of the local tribes. Therefore, to trace out the cultural history of *Char-Khilainee* (a masked dance of the forest dwelling Rabhas) emphasis has been given on the study of local topographical features, physical environment, government forest policy, forest-based traditional tribal economy and its changing pattern. The scope of acculturation and its trend has also been considered. These aspects were instrumental not only in introducing the dance and its propagation but also equally responsible for its total disintegration from cultural scenario.

There are two sections of the Rabhas - Village Rabhas and Jungle Rabhas. *Char-Khilainee*, the Rabha masked dance was exclusively confined to the Jungle Rabhas. Jungle Rabha economy thrived on forest. Physical environment, therefore, influenced their socio-economic life to a great extent. Physical environment, subsistence pattern, acculturation and masked dance were interrelated among the Jungle Rabhas in that isolated pocket. As such, the historical background and the ecological condition of district Jalpaiguri in the past deserve special attention so as to know about the background of the masked dance among the Jungle Rabhas.

III
Formation of District Jalpaiguri

Before 1865 the Duars region of West Bengal was under the administrative control of the Bhutan Government. After the battle of 1864 between the British and the Royal Bhutanese Army 'Shinchula Agreement' was arrived at. According to this agreement the Duars region was detached from Bhutan and it came under the colonial administration. For exercising the administrative control over the newly acquired Duars region, Jalpaiguri sub-division of Rangpur district of Bengal (now Bangladesh) was annexed with Duars forming a new district, Jalpaiguri by name on 1st January, 1869.

The forest areas of Duars located within the district Jalpaiguri is known as Western Duars. It was practically a sparsely populated and isolated zone. This forest clad region was the homeland of the regional tribes. They had little contact with the external world. In the beginning the officials of the colonial administration had no clear idea about this sparsely populated forest belt. Administration was, therefore, hesitant in selecting the appropriate revenue system and the ideal administrative measures for this desolate place. As such, the forest belt of the Duars region (Western Duars) was initially brought under the 'Non-regulation' system. Forest Department was set up for first time. This newly set up Forest Department was entrusted with the responsibility of running the administration of the forest areas. But the remaining part of the district was included within the system of 'Permanent Settlement' under a Deputy Commissioner. Two different administrative and revenue systems were thus introduced initially for the better administration of this newly formed district. As a result the tenural history of the forest areas of Western Duars in particular was different from the remaining part of the district. Not to speak of the forest belt, the ecological condition of Jalpaiguri district in its formative period was so diverse in different pockets that it could be divided into four broad zones on the basis of their physical condition, population distribution and regional economy.

Zone I : Sparsely populated undulating plateau region immediately below the Bhutan Hills.

This region was inhabited by the tribes like Doyoyo, Sonia, Tundu, Khoina, Dukpa, Jaldo, Toto and others. Majority of these tribes came from Bhutan and surrounding areas. They settled down in this region mostly at the instance of the Bhutan rulers to have their services as load-carriers in this mountainous region for carrying out business of Bhutan with North Bengal.

Zone II : Dense forest areas of Western Duars beneath the northern hilly region.

This region was populated mostly by the tribes like Mech, Rabha, Garo, Hajong and others. They were the immigrants from Eastern India, particularly from Assam. These tribes settled down in the jungle belt of Western Duars to lead their traditional socio-economic life peacefully by exploiting the forest resources and practising their age-old slash and burn cultivation.

Zone III :Grass-land interspersed with patchy forest tracts below the dense jungle belt of Duars.

This region was usually counted as no-men's land for insignificant density of population. It was mainly used as pastoral ground. Mostly the Rajbanshi herdsmen annually used to visit the area and put up temporary shelter to spend a couple of months during the lean agricultural season for grazing the cattle of the Hindu and Muslim cultivators of Lower Terai. They used to go back to plain agricultural belt along with their cattle with the approach of agricultural season. When the Rajbanshis used to visit the grass-land area either as herdsman or husbandman, they maintained occasional contact with the forest dwelling tribes for acquiring forest products. Barter system was practised among them for making this transaction.

Zone IV : Lower Terai (an extensive agricultural belt)

Next to grass-land zone was the Lower Terai, an extensive agricultural belt with fertile soil and less rainfall. It was ideal for paddy cultivation. Economy of the region revolved around agriculture. The Hindu and Muslim cultivators along with the marginal Hinduised communities like the Rajbanshis who practised settled cultivation had concentrated themselves in this belt.

Salient features of Duars - the forest clad tribal belt of district Jalpaiguri

Towards the end of the 18th century there were two major geographical areas in Jalpaiguri district - Duars (forest covered land) and Terai (plain land ideal for paddy cultivation). Politically, Duars is referred to as that area lying along the base of the Bhutan Hills. The colonial power took over this part from the Bhutan Government. Geographically, Duars is a flat and low fertile strip of the country running along the foot of the Bhutan Hills and lying between the Bhutan border on the north and Terai, the plain land on the south. On low-lying area which starts from the base of the Bhutan Hills and covers the entire forest belt of district Jalpaiguri extending up to the fringe of Terai, the plain fertile cultivable zone, is known as Duars.

After the introduction of British rule, Duars has been divided into two parts — Eastern Duars (Duars within Goalpara district of Assam) and Western Duars (Duars within Jalpaiguri district of West Bengal). Duars means door (entry point) both in Bengali and Assamese languages. The courses of the main rivers which flow through this region are dried up during winter and summer months. The dried up river beds serve as the entry point and communication channel both the travelling and trade routes from Bhutan to Bengal and vice-versa. The entire geographical area where these entry points are located is called Duars. There are as many as eighteen such major entry points in the entire Duars region. The Jungle Rabhas who practised *Char-Khilainee* (a masked dance) had kept themselves mostly confined to the forest tracts of Western Duars.

2

The Glimpses of Western Duars

On 1st January 1869 the Jalpaiguri district of North Bengal came into existence. It was included within the fold of colonial administration since its very inception. When the British colonial administration extended its network in this region, the forest areas of Western Duars were so sparsely populated that they were excluded from the purview of settlement operations. But the colonial administration came forward to exploit the extremely rich natural resources of the newly acquired region for commercial interest and also for earning revenue in all applicable fields. Therefore a Forest Department was, set up at the earliest to deal with the matters. The newly set up Forest Department took over the administrative control of the forest areas of Western Duars. As such the tenural history of the forest areas was different from the general tenural history of the district.

An effort to exploit the regional forest resources, government turned its attention towards the *Sal* (*Shorea robusta*) forests of Western Duars for the uniqueness of their own. Positive action in this regard was taken up in due course. At the same time the government felt the necessity of plantation of *Sal* saplings in place of the fallen trees to replenish the loss.

Western Duars, a site of the large tracts of *Sal* forest which had been exploited for sometime past, was originally selected as the ideal place for the plantation of *Sal* saplings in a planned way. But the Forest Department had to face much difficulty in executing the plan for want of required manpower.

Adequate manpower was necessary for exploitation of natural resources and manning the *Sal* plantation work. But Western Duars was almost exclusively inhabited by the tribal folk and that too in very limited number. The question of getting the service of the non-tribal population from Lower Terai region (plain agricultural belt) of the district did not arise at all. The non-tribal population from Lower Terai did not dare to come over to the Duars region for multifarious natural hazards, health hazards and many more difficulties. Some of the major problems which stood in the way of attracting the non-tribal population to work in this region were —

1. Numerous river streams and hill present in Duars inundated the area almost every year bringing untold misery to the local inhabitants.

2. Frequent change of the course of the rivers used to bring about unpredictable danger to the settlers.

3. Predominantly forest belt with large tracts of *Sal* forest, heavy grass and reed jungles infested with dangerous wild animals made the life very much risky almost in every step.

4. Proverbially long and persistent rainfall together with frequent attack from leech, insects and venomous snakes made life most miserable during the rainy season.

5. Most unhealthy climatic condition dominated by the endemic diseases like malarious fevers both

remittent and intermittent, with their complications and sequelae together with acute stomach ailments made the life very much difficult to live in this dangerous forest environment.

6. Absence of transportation and communication system, roadways etc., offered little scope for free movement in this region.
7. There was no scope for getting the supply of household articles, commercial commodities, medical help and other essential items which were considered as bare necessity for survival.
8. Opportunity for practising settled cultivation in Duars was practically nil.
9. Political condition of Duars was unstable during the pre-British period. Peace was often disturbed due to frequent fight that took place between the Bhutan king and the rulers of Cooch Behar together with other neighbouring powerful landlords.
10. Over and above, like the European tea planters (private entrepreneurs), the government managed Forest Department had no financial capacity to bring the labour force from Chhotanagpur belt for getting the work done in the forest tracts of Western Duars.

The prevailing dangerous situation stood in the way of attracting the outsiders to come and settle down in the forest belt for taking up the work as forest labourers. So the Forest Department had no other alternative but to depend on the local population living in the forest belt. Before the introduction of colonial administration the forest belt of Duars was almost exclusively inhabited by the tribes like Bhutia, Sherpa, Dukpa, Toto, Kagate, Lepcha, Limbu (immigrants from Nepal, Bhutan and Tibet) together with Mech, Bodo, Rabha, Garo, Hajong, Mug, Mru, Chakma and others who migrated from

Eastern India like Assam and Chittagong Hill tracts. To solve the labour problem at the earliest the Forest Department tried to recruit the labourers from all these communities. Though the selection was made at random, yet the Forest Department was very much conscious in the selection of the community. The department gave special emphasis on those communities who were considered more suitable for carrying out the plantation work. In this respect the tribes who came from Bhutan and surrounding areas were more or less reluctant to give up their traditional load carrying occupation. As their traditional load carrying occupation did not correspond with the forest oriented work, they did not join in desired number in the job offered to them by the Forest Department. The administration, therefore, had to depend on the tribes who migrated from Assam region with special reference to the Rabhas, Garos and Mech. Some of the reasons which prompted the Forest Department to give its attention specially to these communities were —

1. Numerical strength of these tribes were much higher in comparison to the other tribes.
2. Physically the Rabhas, Garos and Mech possessed good health. They were well-built, strong, stout and hard-working.
3. They were very simple, well-behaved and willing to undertake any work assigned to them ungrudgingly.
4. These Assam tribes had been living in the forest environment for generations. They had become the local inhabitants by then. Therefore, they were well accustomed with the regional physical environment and had become immune to the dangerous regional diseases.
5. For their working experience in the forest belt by adopting slash and burn method of cultivation, these

Assam tribes were considered to be the most skilful workers in raising the new *Sal* plantation and also in doing other silvicultural operations including preparation of '*kachcha*' road (muddy road), temporary bridges and their maintenance.

The government had been taken some effective steps for utilising the service of the Assam tribes for *Sal* plantation work. The reasons were obvious. The Assam tribes living in the Duars were nomadic husbandmen. They wondered from place to place in jungle breaking up the virgin soil for cultivation, seldom staying in one place or cultivating the same field for more than two or three years. They then cleared and cultivated a fresh piece of fallow or jungle land. They abandoned the new spot within a few years and returned to the old spot again after the lapse of a couple of years when the soil regained fertility to some extent. Four or five families in general lived together independently in the forest to lead a care-free life style. Until and unless these tribal folk were made to settle down permanently their service could not be utilised for *Sal* plantation work. The Forest Department, therefore adopted certain measures to set up the forest villages.

The settlements which the Forest Department set up in selected spots within the forest areas for accommodation of limited number of tribal families to get the *Sal* plantation work done through them, are referred to as forest villages or forest *bastees*. Though the forest villages were set up in different parts of the forest belt of Western Duars, maximum emphasis was given to the Buxa Forest Division for its geographical position and economic importance. Morever the tribal immigrants from Assam, particularly the Rabhas were mainly confined to this area. Therefore, there was possibility to have the desired number of skilled forest labourers from this belt. As such maximum number of forest villages were set up in the Buxa Forest Division. Being the best forest labourers, the Forest Department gave special attention for persuading the Rabhas to settle down in the forest villages. As a result among the forest villages in the Buxa Division, a few were uni-ethnic, inhabited exclusively by the Rabhas. Among the uni-ethnic Rabha forest villages Poro *Bastee*, Nemati *Bastee*, Shiltong *Bastee*, Indu *Bastee*, Chipra *Bastee* and Barobisha *Bastee* were by far the most conspicuous. Good number of Rabha forest labourers were also living in other forest villages along with the members of other communities. Important Rabha dominated multi-ethnic forest villages under the Buxa Forest Division were Garam *Bastee* (Garo and Rabha), Gadadhar *Bastee* (Garo and Rabha), Sankosh *Bastee* (Garo and Rabha), Balapara *Bastee* (Rabha, Modesia and Nepali), Bengdoba *Bastee* (Rabha, Modesia and Nepali) and Khuntimari *Bastee* (Rabha and Modesia). At present along with the Rabhas and the Garos, the forest *bastees* are occupied by the *Modesia* (a local term meant for denoting the Chhotanagpur tribes) and the Nepalese who are later immigrants. Initially the Assam tribes like Garo, Rabha and others were the earliest settlers of the forest villages in the Buxa Forest Division.

Size of the forest villages

Size of a forest *bastee* usually depended on the volume of work. A *bastee* was initially start with a limited number of families. With the increase of the volume of work, more and more families were included from time to time making it a bigger one. Initially there was only one *bastee* at Poro. As the numerical strength of the population increased and the volume of work sufficiently augmented, necessity for the extension of Poro *Bastee* was keenly felt. Ultimately its second part was established. Now there are two distinct segments of Poro *Bastee* situated approximately one kilometre apart. They are known as North Poro *Bastee* and South Poro *Bastee* of which North Poro *Bastee* is the old one. Poro *Bastee* is a uni-ethnic forest village exclusively inhabited by the Rabhas. It is situated in the Poro Beat of the Buxa Forest Division under Kalchini Police Station of Alipurduar sub-division of the district Jalpaiguri.

Setting up of a forest village

The Forest Department used to take successive steps to set up a forest village. Initially the department selected an area for plantation. It was next calculated the manpower to be required for executing the plantation work in the specified area. Number of families was selected accordingly. As the tribal folk were mostly unwilling to leave their own villages, the selected families were more or less forcibly shifted from their own settlement to the forest village. On behalf of the Forest Department huts were constructed in a predetermined place close to the plantation site for the accommodation of the selected families. The huts had tin roof and they were erected on raised wooden platforms for protection from wild animals. Only a hut was given to the family of a registered worker. The area of the hut was often found smaller in comparison to the number of family members. But the Forest Department used to maintain a standard measurement whether the family was big or small. The department had no responsibility towards the unregistered individuals although they were the offsprings of the registered labourers. The housing arrangement on the spot was made mostly in a row so that the labourers could live close to each other for conveniently taking up the plantation work collectively.

Planning of a Rabha *bastee* was drawn up keeping in view some of the basic considerations. For the convenience of frequently coming and going to keep constant watch the Rabha settlement was invariably set up very close to the plantation field. The field was under constant threat from the wildlife with special reference to the elephants and the wild boars. The Rabhas mostly cultivated '*Vadai* Paddy' in the plantation field. This variety of paddy was really a palatable item of food to the elephants. Therefore, the herds of elephant used to invade the field when the paddy matured. Due to invasion of elephant in the field, not only the paddy was destroyed, but also the *Sal* saplings were damaged. So, it was of common interest for both the Rabhas and the forest officials to get rid of the activities of the hostile elephants. In view of this fact, the Forest Department and the Jungle Rabhas preferred to set up the forest *bastee* very close to the plantation field so that they could collectively drive away the intruding animals at the earliest opportunity. Moreover the Rabha forest workers used to live in the midst of the forest infested with dangerous wild life. They had no sophisticated arms for their protection. They used only their traditional weapons — spears, sticks, bows and arrows. At the same time the Rabhas regularly cleared the jungle by putting up collective organised labour. Therefore, for their protection from wild animals and also for the convenience of organising collective labour the Rabha huts were built up in a row at a very close proximity to one another. This arrangement also helped the forest officials to supervise all the activities of the labourers from close quarter.

Nature of work of the forest labourers

According to Mal Singh Rabha, oldest man of the Poro *bastee* the condition of forest was different before the setting up of the forest *bastees*. Compact tracts of *Sal* tree grew up only after the systematic introduction of *Sal* plantation. Before the plantation work was introduced the *Sal* trees were definitely there in the forest, but they were scatteredly distributed. In between the *Sal* trees there were thick undergrowth, unwanted trees and cane bushes. The contractors offered their bids only for the costly woody plants like *Sal* and others. Generally they used to cut down these trees during the winter months and removed them for transportation elsewhere leaving behind the other unwanted plants of the forest in place. It was the responsibility of the Rabha forest labourers to clean those unwanted plants to make the place ready for plantation and cultivation work. It was really a tough job. With the help of the cutting tools like scythe (*gog*) and axe (*basi*), the Rabhas used to clean the jungles. Their work was not only confined to the cleaning of the jungles but also they had to uproot the lower part of the trunks (one or two feet above the ground level) which were left behind in the field after the felling of the woody plants. The discarded jungle components and the uprooted tree trunks were left behind on the spot to be dried up for burning at a later period. There were many varieties of thorny plants and creepers growing scatteredly in the forest. The Rabha labourers, therefore, used wooden footwear while working in the jungle. They also carried with them tobacco, pipe and stone pieces for making fire which they either kept in a side bag or in the fold of their napkin. Smoking was essential to energise the labourers for putting up hard labour involved in clearing the jungle.

Day to day work in the plantation field was looked after by the Beat Officer. Occasionally the higher officer from Rajabhatkhaowa used to come for supervising the work on the spot. There was no road linking of Poro with Rajabhatkhaowa. So he had to travel by riding on an elephant. All the members of each Rabha family had to remain present in an allocated field on the day of special inspection. The higher officer himself inspected the individual plot and gave necessary instruction to the allottee. If any family failed to put up work satisfactorily, its members were punished in different ways including physical torture. If necessary, a family could be expelled from the *bastee.*

A leader was selected from each forest *bastee* for communicating the instructions of the Forest Department to the forest labourers in time and in clear-cut manner. He was known as 'Mandal'. It was through the Mandal Beat Officer used to send the massages of the Forest Department to the common labourers and also enquired from him about their activities.

There was certain procedure followed for cleaning the jungle. The usual practice was that towards the end of rainy season the Forest Department used to decide which part of the forest would be sold out to the contractors. Generally during the winter months the contractors used to cut down the stipulated big trees and took away the load from the jungle leaving behind the ordinary plants, cane-bush and the undergrowth. The idea behind the distribution of land among the *bastee* dwellers was to get the left-over jungle cleaned by them and to replenish the loss by planting the *Sal* saplings on the spot. It was the responsibility of the forest officials to distribute the plots of land among the *bastee* dwellers. The area to be allotted to a family depended on its working capacity. The working capacity of the family again rested on the number of available working hands. Both male and female members of the family used to participate in the work. The function of each family was to clean the jungle area allocated to it and also to plant the Sal saplings in that space. They could cultivate different varieties of crop and vegetable in the plantation field for their sustenance. But no payment was made to them for plantation work. By allowing them to cultivate in the reserved forest the forest officials forced the Rabha workers to work free of cost. There was no separate land for cultivation within the plantation area. They had to cultivate only in the patches of land cleaned by them for *Sal* plantation. Therefore, the plantation of *Sal* saplings, cultivation of crops and production of vegetables were done simultaneously in the same field. The Forest Department entrusted the responsibility of *Sal* plantation work with the Rabhas in view of their cultivation technique (slash and burn) which had some basic similarity with *Sal* plantation work. As such there was no problem in carrying out both the types of work in the same field. One category of work used to help directly or indirectly in carrying out the work of other.

The Rabha forest workers were permitted to practise their traditional cultivation technique in the plantation field with definite end in view. It was then believed that the *Sal* saplings could not grow properly under a matured *Sal* tree within a radius of approximately ten feet or so. The matured tree used to release certain excreta from its body and this excreta made the soil uncongenial for the growth of the saplings. This harmful effect could be removed by the heat treatment of the soil. Hence the undergrowth, dry leaves, uprooted free-trunks and other discarded plant products were burnt directly on the surface of the soil. The slash and burn method of cultivation as practised by the tribal folk was, therefore, allowed to practise for removing this injurious effect of the soil paving the way for successful plantation of *Sal* saplings in the *Sal* plantation field. At the same time fertility of the soil could be improved with the help of the ash of the burnt undergrowth, dry leaves and the discarded branches of the trees whether big or small. The vacant space in between two adjacent *Sal* trees or saplings (approximately 6 to 10 feet or so) which was deliberately kept for the interest of the growing plants was utilised for cultivation. In such short space there was no scope for plough cultivation. For the convenience of the *Sal* plantation, slash and burn type of cultivation was practised in the plantation field. Therefore, instead of plough the Rabha forest labourers used a small curved iron implement (*bhou*) which was hand operated. It was ideally suited for cultivation in the *Sal* plantation field. This implement was used both for turning up the soil and carrying out the dibbling work. This specific implement was used not to hurt the root of the saplings in the process of preparation of soil for cultivation in the plantation field.

The Rabhas practised mixed type of cultivation. They produced paddy, cash crop (cotton) and vegetables in the same plantation field. Sometimes the seeds were planted by dibbling. Occasionally the seeds of different crops were mixed and sown by broadcasting along with the paddy. Paddy was the principal crop followed by the cash crop (cotton). Among other items mustard, arum, ginger, turmeric and tobacco were conspicuous. Familiar vegetables were pumpkin, gourd, lady's finger, chilli, brinjal etc.

Cultivation played a very important role in the economic life of the Rabhas. Rice was their staple food. They lived in deep interior of the forest belt. They had no connection with the market economy. They used paddy for entering into barter to procure metallic objects and daily necessities from the visiting petty rural vendors locally known as 'Baladia'. Use of cash money was almost out of question. They prepared their own garments out of cotton produced in their own field. Mustard, another agricultural product was liberally used in cooking. In one way or another the Rabhas engaged themselves in the field through out the year both as forest labourers and cultivators.

The forest dwelling Rabhas used two categories of land for cultivation. They were (1) land allocated to them by the Forest Department outside the plantation field particularly for cultivation and (2) available space found in the plantation field. In cultivation, the Rabha forest labourers gave much importance to paddy. Though they cultivated both the *ausdhan* (*bitirmai*) and the *amandhan* (*rawmai*) but they preferred the *aus* variety. There were two varieties of *ausdhan* — one (summer variety), sown in February-March and second, (the autumn variety) the most important one sown in March-April and reaped in August and September. The second variety was popularly known as '*Bhadai aus*'. It was named after *Bhadra*, the Bengali month when this category of paddy was harvested. Generally, *Bhadai aus* was cultivated in high land. It required lesser quantity of water to grow. Heavy monsoon rain of Duars was adequate enough to meet its requirement. Less fertile high arable land (*Hatong*) of plantation field in Western Duars had the ideal condition for the cultivation of this coarse variety of paddy. The Rabhas used to face severe food crisis during autumn. The *Bhadai paddy* brought about much relief to them at this critical juncture. Hence the plantation labourers gave much emphasis on *Bhadai paddy* which served as their principal crop. They used to cultivate *amandhan* (*hemtidhan*) in the specially allocated cultivable land outside the plantation field. This variety of paddy was sown in the month of *Shraban-Bhadra* (July-August) and harvested in the month of *Agrahayan-Pous* (December-January).

The Rabha forest labourers also depended upon forest products particularly in the crisis period during rainy season. Hunting, fishing and gathering were their secondary subsistence activities. They used to procure forest products whenever opportunity arose. Therefore, both cultivation and gathering of forest resources were integrally associated with their economic life.

Advantages and disadvantages of life in the forest villages

1. The economic life of the forest *bastee* dwellers underwent radical change when they were uprooted from their own settlement.

2. They lost the right of carrying out cultivation freely in the forest.

3. They were permitted to cultivate in the plantation field and that too, in limited area.

4. Only advantage they derived in the new situation was that they could follow their traditional cultivation technique (slash and burn) in the plantation field but in much smaller scale.

5. They could also cultivate outside the plantation field in the land allotted to the authorised villagers. Area of land allotted to the registered villagers varied in respect of wet (plain forest) and dry (hill forest) cultivation areas. In wet cultivation areas each household was allotted with 2.5 acres of land, whereas in dry cultivation areas only 1.5 acres of land were allotted to each household.

6. The forest *bastee* dwellers were living in the same forest environment as before. They could, therefore, carry out their traditional hunting-gathering economy in case of necessity. Being the forest labourers they did enjoy special advantage in this regard.

7. Free shelter was given to them. The Forest Department also arranged for repairing of huts of the labourers in case of necessity.

8. There was no bar in maintaining their traditional socio-religious life.

9. First and foremost concern of the forest labourers was the plantation work. They could perform their own work whether cultivation or otherwise, only if time permitted them to do so outside the scope of plantation work.

10. The honorarium in any form was not paid to them for carrying out the plantation work. They had to put up this enforced forest related work free of cost.

11. They had no ownership right on the land allocated to them for cultivation. Land was allotted to the forest labourers only as service *jagir* (rent free) for sustenance of their families. They had to sign an agreement for ensuring the supply of labour for the forest authorities. The forest labourers could only utilise the land so long their names were there in the labour registration record. They had no right to sell or mortgage the land at any point of time.

12. The plantation labourers had to perform the plantation work to the best of their ability under the strict surveillance of the forest officials.

13. Severe punishment was imposed on a worker's family if it failed to put up the assigned responsibility. Punishment even in terms of physical torture was perpetrated on its members.

14. The forest labourers lost their freedom. Their movement was mostly restricted to the plantation areas. They were not allowed to leave the forest village. To lead their traditional way of life any more, was out of question. They survived in the forest villages completely at the mercy of the forest officials and their economic life was fully controlled by them.

15. Being cut off from the main stream and living in almost inaccessible forest belt, the forest officials treated the tribal plantation labourers like slaves.

As a result, they were the worst victims of deprivation and exploitation in comparison to others living outside the forest villages.

General impact of colonial administration on the tribes of Western Duars

Forests laws imposed on the forest belt of Western Duars brought an overall change in the economic life of the forest dwelling tribes.

1. The colonial administration imposed its right on all natural resources mainly to earn revenue from all possible sources.

2. The local tribes lost their age-old right to freely exploit the natural resources.

3. The very basis of their economy which revolved around shifting cultivation was threatened.

4. The Forest Department in particular had tried to impose forcibly the government right on natural resources so that the local tribes instead of searching for alternative livelihood, might join the organised labour force meant for *Sal* plantation.

5. Deviation in economic front brought about a significant change among the local tribes. They initially had settled down in Western Duars for enjoying economic freedom and leading a peaceful life. But when both the aspects were being threatened from new administration, many of them preferred to leave the forest areas in search of new habitation.

Impact on tribal distribution

Majority of the tribes living in the northern hilly region had left earlier and settled down in Bhutan when the Bhutan ruler had handed over the region to the colonial power. Under the changed situation, the remaining groups also left the region to find suitable place for rehabilitation elsewhere. The landed properties which they left behind were either given for converting into tea gardens or remained fallow to develop automatically into a forest land in due course.

Under the prevailing condition the Assam tribes were in two minds. One section remained in the forest inspite of hardship. This section joined in the government organised labour force for *Sal* plantation. Another section left the forest zone and settled down in the villages of the fringe areas surrounding the forest belt to lead a settled villages life. The rearrangement of tribal distribution in Western Duars as a result of the government forest policy paved the way for steady acculturation among the hitherto secluded tribal population of Western Duars.

3

The Context of Acculturation

Rabhas section Rabhas who had left the forest belt to settle down outside this ecological setting, started living around the Rajbanshi villages in the pastoral zone. During the pre-British days the Rabhas while living in the jungle had the opportunity to coming in casual contact with the Rajbanshis of the pastoral zone, in connection with commercial transaction of jungle products. They had no contact with any other community living outside the jungle belt. So immediately after leaving their jungle habitat, the Rabha families preferred to live around the Rajbanshi villages situated close to the jungle areas. It led to divide the Rabhas into two sections — forest dwelling Rabhas and village dwelling Rabhas, now commonly referred to as Jungle Rabhas and Village Rabhas.

Forest policy of the colonial administration could not make any impact on the Hindu cultivators. They were living in the agricultural zone of Lower Terai as before. To avoid the menace of the wildlife and dangerous diseases of Duars they even avoided the bordering zone of the forest belt right from the very beginning. They had kept themselves mostly confined to the middle and the lower part of Terai region. The Hindus had, therefore, no direct contact with the tribal population of Duars and did not play any direct role in acculturation process.

Background of acculturation

(a) The Hindus and the Rajbanshis

In the agricultural belt of Lower Terai the Hinduised Rajbanshis, one of the dominant communities of North Bengal who were settled cultivators, used to live in the vicinity of the Hindu villages since a long time. At the same time a section of the Rajbanshi population was also living scatteredly in the pastoral zone of Upper Terai just outside the tribal dominated forest zone.

The Hindus considered the Rajbanshis as an inferior community both socially and culturally. They were economically backward as well. The Rajbanshis for their subsistence used to work for the Hindu families in different fronts primarily as domestic servants, cow-boys, agricultural labourers and occasionally played the role of share-croppers. Apart from the agricultural front, they put up menial labour of different nature in the Hindu villages. The Rajbanshi cow-boys took upon themselves the responsibility of grazing the cattle of the Hindu and the Muslim cultivators for months together in the pastoral zone in exchange of remuneration either in cash or kind. The Rajbanshis mainly lived outside the Hindu villages to maintain social distance but in close proximity to the Hindus for the convenience of performing economic activities.

Due to intimate contact for over a long period of time, there was adequate scope of acculturation among the Hindus and the Rajbanshis. But the Rajbanshis were really orthodox and conservative. They had firm faith in their own traditional culture. They maintained their social system as a water-tight compartment. So initially the impact of acculturation was not so clearly witnessed in their cultural life except in the sphere of their religious beliefs and practices. In the process of maintaining economic co-operation the Rajbanshis accepted a few selected benevolent Hindu deities in their religious life without disturbing their own animistic thoughts. The addition of powerful Hindu deities in their religious life was undoubtedly an impact of acculturation. Though it was a very slow process, but the impact of acculturation which started initially with economic co-operation, followed by the acceptance of the Hindu deities, made deep penetration in other spheres of their cultural life, through the long period of time uplifting the Rajbanshis from a tribe to a scheduled caste as their status stands to-day.

Acculturation between the Rajbanshis and the Rabhas

The Rajbanshis had preliminary contact with the jungle dwelling Rabhas during the pre-British period. This contact used to take place in the fringe was areas of the forest belt and the pastoral zone. Not only the Rajbanshi cow-boys, but also the petty Rajbanshi farmers living scatteredly in the pastoral zone, occasionally met the Rabhas of the jungle belt to collect the jungle products on barter. They utilised those materials to enter into commercial transaction with the people of the agricultural belt of Lower Terai to derive some economic benefit. The initial stray contact of the pre-British period became a regular feature during the British period.

A section of the Rabhas left their forest habitat to get rid of the forest rules imposed by the colonial administration. Initially outside the forest areas they settled down in the pastoral zone and subsequently penetrated into the agricultural belt. The Rabhas living in the jungle areas during the pre-British period had no contact with any other community practising settled cultivation except the Rajbanshis though it was a marginal contact. They considered the Rajbanshis culturally superior to them and tried to follow them faithfully in their economic life. So the uprooted Rabhas set up their habitation around the Rajbanshi villages in the new situation.

Many of the Rajbanshi villages were situated in the fringe area of the Lower Terai adjacent to the pastoral zone interspersed with patchy forest tracts. The Rajbanshis had selected the area for simultaneously carrying out the plough cultivation and also for practising the pastoral economy. The situation was ideal for the newly settled Rabhas as well. Outside the forest zone, the Rabhas had no way out but to take up the settled cultivation for subsistence. Vast open field suitable for paddy cultivation was available all around the Rajbanshi villages of the fringe areas. Besides they had to learn the settled cultivation technique from the Rajbanshis. The Rabhas also initially preferred the fringe areas for setting up their settlement. They wanted to utilise the nearby forest tracts for practising their traditional hunting-gathering economy and also to meet their estranged friends and relatives living in the jungle. On the other hand the Rajbanshis came forward to co-operate with the Rabhas to utilise them as menial force in their agricultural operation and also to get the regular supply of forest products through them. By living in close proximity, both the Rajbanshis and the Village Rabhas derived mutual benefit. The Village Rabhas initially had no scope of coming in contact with the Hindus. On the contrary they had regular and close contact with the Rajbanshis. In the process of acculturation the Rajbanshis acquired the Hindu cultural elements directly from the Hindus. But the Village Rabhas on their part derived those elements through the Rajbanshis.

Cultural transmission between the Village Rabhas and the Jungle Rabhas

The Jungle Rabhas never had any sort of contact with the Hindus. They had only superficial casual contact with the Rajbanshis for minor economic transaction. Such contact was not adequate enough for acculturation. But the Village Rabhas initially maintained more or less regular contact with the Jungle Rabhas to meet their friends and relatives and also to acquire forest products through them. It was through the Village Rabhas, the Forest Rabhas for the first time came to know about the Hindu cultural elements. But they had no scope of implementing those concepts into practice, as they were living in the interior of the jungle belt with no scope of communication with the external world.

Rural-based cultures of all the communities — the Hindus, the Muslims, the Rajbanshis and the tribes in the newly formed District Jalpaiguri were almost static. With no communication facility worth mentioning they had little scope of communication with the external world. They kept themselves strictly confined within their own regional territory. Self-sufficient village economy was the order of the day. Rural-based traditional simple technology was in vogue. Illiteracy reigned supreme. Scope of market economy and availability of commercial commodities were out of question. Rural societies were extremely conservative. They kept them practically confined within themselves. As a result acculturation took place at an extremely slow pace. Speed of acculturation was so slow that it was not noticeable almost in all fronts barring a few. One of the cultural fronts where acculturation could be traced initially was the religion. In the backdrop of such acculturation process during the early part of colonial administration, origin of the socio-religious masked dance "*Char-Khilainee*" could be traced among the Jungle Rabhas.

Acculturation in the religious front

'Sakta Cult' in general is very strong among the Hindus of West Bengal. It has further been augmented by the tantric influence of the Mahajana Section of Buddhism. Both the Buddhist tantric influence and the impact of Sakta Cult have made the Bengali Hindus inclined towards the Goddess *Kali*, supreme deity of the Sakta cult. Hence, Goddess *Kali* has been considered as the principal deity of the Hindus. There is no exception in case of the Rajbanshis of North Bengal who are now in Hindu fold and are recognised as one of the scheduled castes in West Bengal. But the earlier authors like Dalton, Risley, Gait, Hamilton and a few others were of opinion that the Rajbanshis were the converted Koches, a dominant tribal group of North Bengal.

In the Tribes and Castes of West Bengal (1953 : 73) Risley mentioned that the Koches are the original inhabitants of Coochbehar and neighbouring areas. Risley describes them as a Dravidian tribe with suspected admixture of Mongolian blood. According to him ethnologically Koches, Rajbanshis and Polia of North Bengal have the same origin and treated Koches as identical with the Rajbanshis. Like the Koches, heavy concentration of the Rajbanshis is also there in North Bengal. The opinion of the earlier scholars suggests that the Rajbanshis had tribal origin though they at present disdain their affiliation to the tribal group. They claim themselves as '*Kshatriya*'.

Rural-based Hindu economy thrives on agriculture. The Rajbanshi economy also rests on the same. The Hindus and the Rajbanshis have been living together in contact situation for generations to have economic co-operation. Therefore, there was scope for rapid acculturation between them. It paved the way for the Rajbanshis to adopt the worship of Goddess *Kali*, one of the major Hindu deities.

Similar trend is witnessed among the Rabhas of North Bengal. Under the influence of the Rajbanshis, a Hinduised community, the Village Rabhas are now inclined towards the Sakta form of Hindu religion. They, therefore, give much importance to the worship of Goddess *Kali*. "The Rabhas perform *Kali Puja* on the new-moon night of the month of *Kartick* (Oct. - Nov.) when the Hindus perform the same *puja*. For this *puja* they purchase earthen effigy of the deity from the local potters, who are *kumor* by caste. The village priest is employed for the *puja*. The procedure of the *puja* is same as is followed by the local Hindus". (Das and Raha, 1967, p. 139).

During the British period there was rather less scope for acculturation between the Jungle Rabhas and the Village Rabhas. They did not maintain direct and regular continuous contact. Their contact was mostly casual. Inspite of the fact, the Village Rabhas were the main source through whom the Jungle Rabhas could know something about the external world.

The Jungle Rabhas lived in the interior of the jungle belt. But the Village Rabhas settled down in the permanent villages of the agricultural zone. The Jungle Rabhas were the forest labourers. On the contrary the Village Rabhas were the settled cultivators. As there was no communicable route in the jungle belt and the nature of profession was entirely different, the two sections of the Rabhas would hardly meet. The Village Rabhas have adopted many of the Hindu cultural elements from the Rajbanshis. As a result significant cultural change has taken place among them. But the Jungle Rabhas being secluded from other communities are still maintaining their traditional cultural pattern to a great extent. So differences in their habitat, subsistence activities, culture pattern and outlook are that the Village Rabhas and the Jungle Rabhas do not even enter into marital relation. Superficial contact takes place only for transaction of Jungle products. In view of the fact traditional cultural life of the Jungle Rabhas could not be sufficiently influenced by the Village Rabhas. The Jungle Rabhas could only come to know a little about the Hindu cultural elements which the Village Rabhas have adopted. But there was no scope for the Jungle Rabhas to implement those ideas into practice in their secluded forest environment. Utmost they could borrow an idea from the Village Rabhas and could also implement this borrowed idea only in their own way to make use of it within the scope of their forest environment. Introduction of '*Char-Khilainee*' dance was one of such attempts.

It was through the casual contact with the Village Rabhas the Jungle Rabhas not only got the idea of worshipping the Goddess *Kali*, but also came to know about her very nature, iconographic form and the benefit of offering worship to her. Undoubtedly they borrowed those ideas but could not implement them in their secluded forest environment. The Village Rabhas worship the earthen images and utilise the service of the village priest and also follow the Hindu rituals. It was not possible for the Jungle Rabhas to get the supply of earthen image of the deity. No priest was available for offering worship. Almost in all respects they failed to fulfil the demand of the essential items necessary for performing Her worship. But at the same time they could not give up the idea of appeasing the deity for the sake of well-being of the community. With a view to derive Her blessing they tried to give Goddess *Kali* due recognition in their own way within their limitation.

Reason for the acceptance of the concept of Goddess *Kali*

The Jungle Rabhas lived in the interior of the jungle. They did not have the capacity to combat the natural hazards nor they had effective weapons to protect themselves from dangerous wild life living all around. Their life were threatened all the time from natural hazards, wildlife and dangerous diseases. Receiving any external help for the purpose was out of question. They, therefore, used to live in constant danger in their forest environment. The Jungle Rabhas usually sought the supernatural help for their well-being and safety. They considered the Village Rabhas superior to them both from economical and cultural point of view. From the Village Rabhas they came to know about Goddess *Kali*. She is believed to be the deity who controls the safety and well-being of the people. When the Jungle Rabhas became aware that the Village Rabhas had adopted the worship of this deity for their safety, security and well-being, they did not hesitate to adopt the idea of appeasing the Goddess *Kali* with the intention of seeking Her blessings for their protection, prosperity and happiness.

Steps taken up by the Jungle Rabhas to overcome their limitations

In the forest environment the Jungle Rabhas had no scope of offering worship to Goddess *Kali* as the Village Rabhas did. But they found out an alternative idea. The Jungle Rabhas prepared a replica of the Goddess in their own way. They are very much efficient in bamboo plaiting work. They, therefore, within the scope of their technological skill gave definite shape to a bamboo plaited structure to convert it into a mask of the deity. The Village Rabhas worship the full figure clay image of Goddess *Kali*. On the contrary the Jungle Rabhas gave up the concept of full figure. They took up only the facial portion. Facial features of the Goddess were depicted on the mask to make it Her replica.

The Jungle Rabhas had shown their innovative idea in depicting the facial features of the deity. As per the

Brahmanical concept which the Village Rabhas have adopted, Goddess *Kali* is a female deity with dark black complexion. Angry facial expression is another salient feature of the image of the deity. Her angry expression is expressed through widely open and expanded eyes, protruded tongue, spreadout lips and exposed frontal teeth. The Jungle Rabhas depicted all these features on the mask in their own way. Instead of black they used white as the background colour of the mask. Angry mood of the deity was depicted simply by painting the widely open eyes and the exposed frontal teeth. A piece of skin (goat) was used for depicting the protruded tongue. They used only two colours - black and red for depicting the facial features on the mask against its white body colour. In their forest environment they could use only two or three colours. Among them red and black were by far the most conspicuous. The Jungle Rabhas used them for depicting the facial features. These two dark colours do not come out conspicuously against the dark black background. Therefore, they used white as the background or body colour of the mask so as to depict the facial features conspicuously with red and black.

The Jungle Rabhas did not offer any worship to the mask. As an alternative, they developed their own conception to give religious string to it as a replica of Goddess *Kali*. They believed that the spirit of the Goddess used to harbour in the mask. Spirit possession of the mask took place immediately after the painting of the eyes. Therefore, a Rabha craftsman who used to prepare the mask painted the eyes at the last moment when it was finally ready for use. Religious sanction was accorded to the mask as soon as the eyes were depicted. A mask with religious sanction required constant care and supervision for maintaining its sanctity. Therefore, the mask of Goddess *Kali* was prepared just one day in advance of its functional application. It was cut into pieces and thrown away in the running water of the river as soon as its function was over. The idea behind this destruction was not to dishonour the sanctity of the mask in any way when not in use.

Possible origin of the conception of mask and masked dance

The Jungle Rabhas might have borrowed the conception of mask, masked dance and the spirit possession of mask from the Rajbanshi, the Desi and the Polia communities of North Bengal through the Village Rabhas. The Desi and Polia are believed to be the two other subdivisions of the Rajbanshis. They are all Hinduised agriculturists. All these communities perform worship of Goddess *Kali* immediately after ploughing, sowing and transplantation, the first session of paddy cultivation, expecting the blessing of the Goddess for better agricultural production. It is generally performed in the month of July. The worship is organised collectively either by the inhabitants of a big village or a number of small villages. There is no specific date for the worship. It is according to the convenience of the villagers, the village elders select the date. The worship is performed in a stipulated sacred place of the village. Subscription is collected from the villagers to meet the expenditure. The villagers organise a masked dance on the date of worship to celebrate the occasion. It is through this dance they try to appease the deity and also to entertain the villagers. It is known as '*Gamira Dance*'. Mostly the masks of the Hindu mythological gods and goddesses and also the demons are used on this occasion. But two ordinary wooden masks - masks of an old man and an old lady, two comical figures are extensively used in the dance to entertain the audience. They have no specific choreography. By their gesture and posture they make the people laugh. The mask of Goddess *Kali* and also the mask of '*Shiknidhal*' (evil spirit) receive special treatment on the occasion. The people believe that these two masks may possess the influence of the Goddess and the evil spirit respectively at the time of performance. Among the Desi and the Polia communities, '*Debanshi*', a village priest who is also an expert in dispelling the evil influence of the spirits, always remains present on the dancing ground. He keeps himself ready all the time with sacred water in hand to dispel the evil influence of the spirit if the situation so demands. Thus, the use of mask, masked dance and concept of spirit are very much there among the Rajbanshi and the two other communities of North Bengal (Desi and Polia). The Village Rabhas have also not been able to come out of this influence. They use a bear mask (*Mapar-Char*) at the time of collection of subscription, for organising collectively the worship of Goddess *Kali* in the village. This mask is made out of gourd shell and the dance associated with the bear mask is known as '*Makpar-Basini*'. When the Jungle Rabhas had borrowed the concept of Goddess *Kali* basically from the Rajbanshis through the Village Rabhas, it is probable that they might have also derived the concepts of masks, masked dance and spirit possession of masks from the Rajbanshis through the Village Rabhas.

The Rajbanshis, the Desi andPolia - all the three communities liberally use wooden masks of an old man and an old lady in connection with the masked dance *(Gamira)* associated with their religious festival (*Kali puja*). But these two masks are purely secular in their functional role. They are put to use exclusively to entertain the audience present on the occasion. Similarly the Jungle Rabhas, a regional tribe also introduced a wooden mask of a male individual in their *Char-Khilainee* dance. It had no ritual value connected with it. It was just an auxiliary item introduced in the socio-religious performance (*Char-Khilainee* dance). Its presence or absence had nothing to do with this masked dance. Peculiar dress of the dancer, curious shape of his stick (held in hand) and unethical choreography had nothing to do with the ritual part of the dance. It was only meant for entertaining the assembled gathering. This shows that the Jungle Rabhas had also borrowed the idea of introducing a masked dancer exclusively for entertaining the assembled gathering at the time of performing their *Char-Khilainee* dance as the Rajbanshi, Desi and Polia do in connection with their *Gamira* dance. It is thus apparent that during the early part of colonial administration acculturation in religious front among the Hindus, the scheduled castes and the scheduled tribes of Western Duars took place in the following order :

Hindus → Rajbanshis → Village Rabhas → Jungle Rabhas

The Hindus were dominant in the Lower Terai region. The Rajbanshi, a scheduled caste who used to live in contact situation with the Hindus, borrowed the Hindu cultural elements through the process of acculturation. The Rajbanshis were dominant in the Upper Terai. The Village Rabhas, a local tribe used to live in good number in the immediate neighbourhood of the Rajbanshis of this region. Therefore, it was through acculturation the Village Rabhas got the opportunity of borrowing the Hindu cultural elements from the Rajbanshis. The Village Rabhas on their part had rather casual contact with the Jungle Rabhas of the Duars belt. It offered the Jungle Rabhas of Western Duars some scope to adopt atleast superficially certain ideas about the Hindu cultural elements from the Village Rabhas.

The result of acculturation which initially took place in Lower Terai (between the Hindus and the Rajbanshis) was passed on to the Village Rabhas of the Upper Terai. The Village Rabhas on their part passed it on to the Jungle Rabhas of the Duars region. Thus the process of acculturation which was started in Lower Terai ultimately reached the forest belt of Western Duars by passing through the Upper Terai. The Rajbanshi played the leading role for successful implementation of the acculturation process. They had adopted the cultural elements directly from the Hindus and passed them on to the Village Rabhas who on their part handed those borrowed cultural elements over to the Jungle Rabhas though in much diffused form.

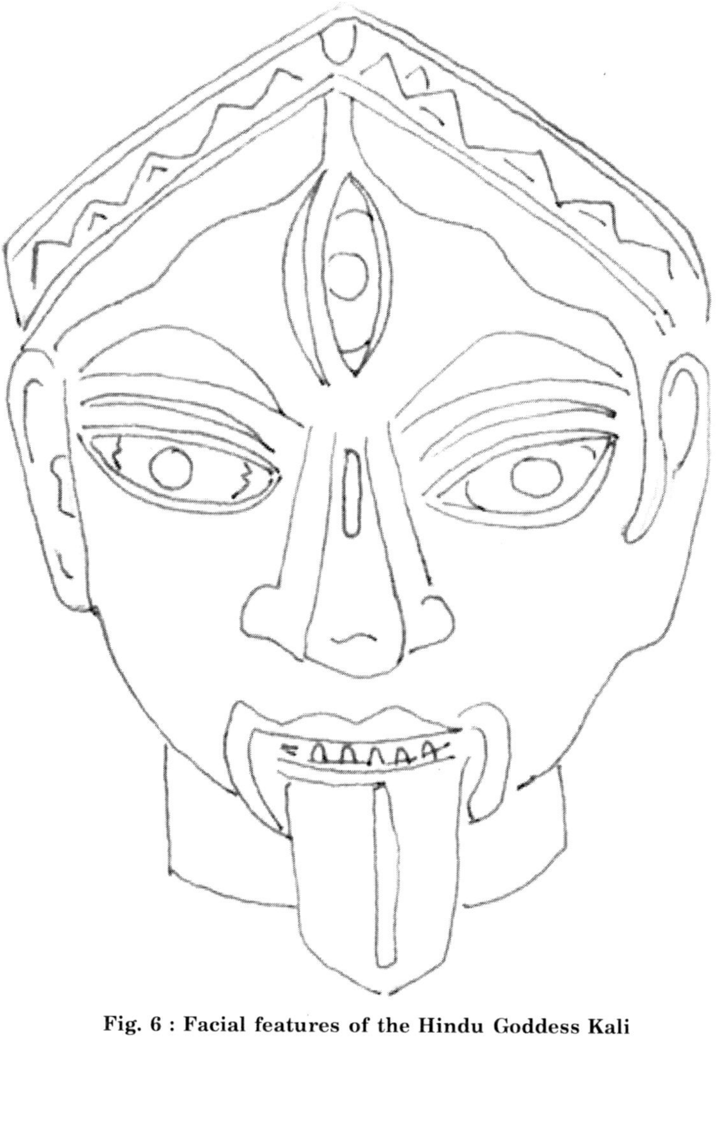

Fig. 6 : Facial features of the Hindu Goddess Kali

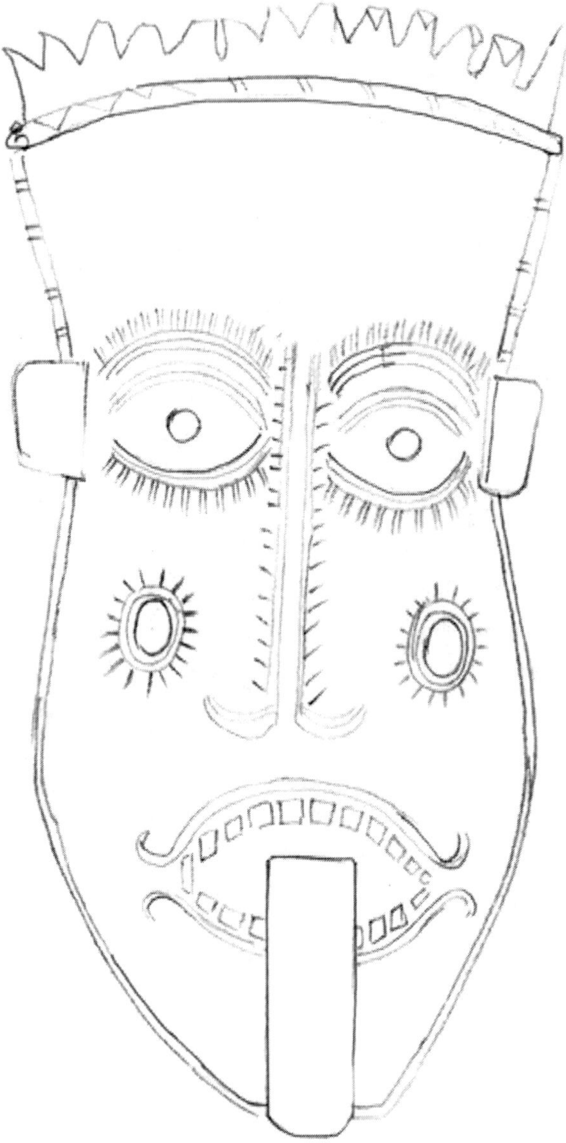

Fig. 7 : Facial features of the Rabha mask of Goddess Kali

4

The Structural Features of Masks

Introduction

Mask is actually an artificial covering over the face. Different kinds of materials such as wood, paper-board, paper-pulp, metal, clay, bark and many more are used for making the masks. Facial features are in general depicted on the outer surface of the covering either by way of carving or by painting. Occasionally partial modelling work is also executed.

Both the sections of the Rabha (Village Rabha and Jungle Rabha) used mask in their respective dance performance. The Village Rabhas used the mask of a bear in their *Makbar Basini* dance. On the contrary the Jungle Rabhas utilise the mask of Goddess Kali in their *Char-Khilainee* dance. Besides these two categories, the Jungle Rabhas also use a wooden mask. It is the mask of a common man. They have adopted the wooden mask from the Rajbanshis. The Rajbanshis, with special reference to the Deshis and the Polias, use wooden masks of an old man (*Bura*) and an old woman (*Buri*) in their *Gamira* dance performance only for entertaining the assembled gathering by jesting. The role of jester is very much appreciated by the local people. Similarly

Table 4.1

Common name	*Name in Rabha language*	*Sphere of use*	*Users*
Mask of a bear	*Mapar-Char*	1. Used as principal mask in *Makbar Basini* dance. 2. Used in *Char-Khilainee* dance as an auxiliary item.	1. Village Rabhas regularly 2. Forest Rabhas casually
Mask of a common man	*Char-Pagal*	Used in *Char-Khilainee* dance as an auxiliary item	Jungle Rabhas
Mask of Goddess *Kali* (*Chandi*)	*Char-Gog*	Used in *Char-Khilainee* dance as the principal mask	Jungle Rabhas

the Rabhas have also adopted a wooden mask of a common man only for entertaining the on-lookers by playing the role of a jester and demonstrating posture of various forms leading to caricature. As such, it has no attachment with any specific dance. It may be used in any dance where there is scope for offering entertainment by way of jesting and demonstrating interesting postures. From this point of view the Jungle Rabhas occasionally use wooden mask of an old man in their *Char-Khilainee* dance.

The Rabhas in their language mention the wooden mask as *Char-Pagal*. The mask which is made of bamboo strips and assumes the facial form of Goddess *Kali,* a Hindu deity, is named as *Char-Gog* in Rabha language. The Rabhas in their language refer to the bear-mask made of gourd-shell as *Mapar-Char*. Particulars of the bamboo stripped mask of Goddess *Kali* are very much needed to have an idea about the technical skills aesthetic sense and religious conception of the Jungle Rabhas. The gourd-shell mask (bear-mask) is also infrequently used in the *Char-Khilainee* dance as a ceremonial one. As such the Jungle Rabhas use all the three categories of mask in their masked dance. Among them the bamboo made mask is the principal one. Other two are simply auxiliary items. In brief, the particulars of these masks are as follows.

Descriptive Account

1. Bamboo stripped mask

Name : A mask made of bamboo strips is mentioned as *Char-Gog* in Rabha language. From its structural form the neighbouring communities call it as mask of *Kali*. The Rabhas often refer to it as the *Chandi* mask.

Locality : Bamboo stripped mask is confined to the Jungle Rabhas living in the forest *bastees* of Jalpaiguri district in Duars region.

Makers : Jungle Rabha craftsmen.

User : Jungle Rabhas living in the forest *bastees.*

Constituent materials : Bamboo, white cloth, cotton thread, a piece of wood and goat-skin.

Size : There is no specific size of the mask. In general it varies between 12 to 15 inches in length and its breadth ranges between 8 to 10 inches or so.

Description : Thin strips of bamboo are plaited to prepare the basic structure. The basic bamboo stripped structure on its part assumes more or less the form of a winnowing fan. Margin of its upper end is straight, whereas its lower margin takes more or less an elliptical form. A sheet of worn-out white cloth is used to cover the entire upper surface of the flat bamboo structure. It remains adhered to the bamboo plaited surface by way of stitching with white thread all along the margin. For the protection of the free margin of the bamboo stripped structure two strips of bamboo around one cm in breadth are used. The margin of the plaited structure is kept concealed between these two strips so that any part of the free margin may not remain exposed. These two strips are firmly tied together at regular interval so that they remain firmly in desired position for discharging their function. Goat skin is used to give definite shape to the protruded tongue and the ears. This variety of skin is also used to decorate all along the upper free margin of the mask. Lime is used to apply a coating of white colour on the entire dorsal surface of the bamboo plaited structure. A piece of wood placed at appropriate position stands for nasal bridge. It is by way of painting with black and red — eye, eye-brows, lips, teeth, decorative designs have been depicted. The painting assumes the form of juvenile work, an artistic output of immature hand.

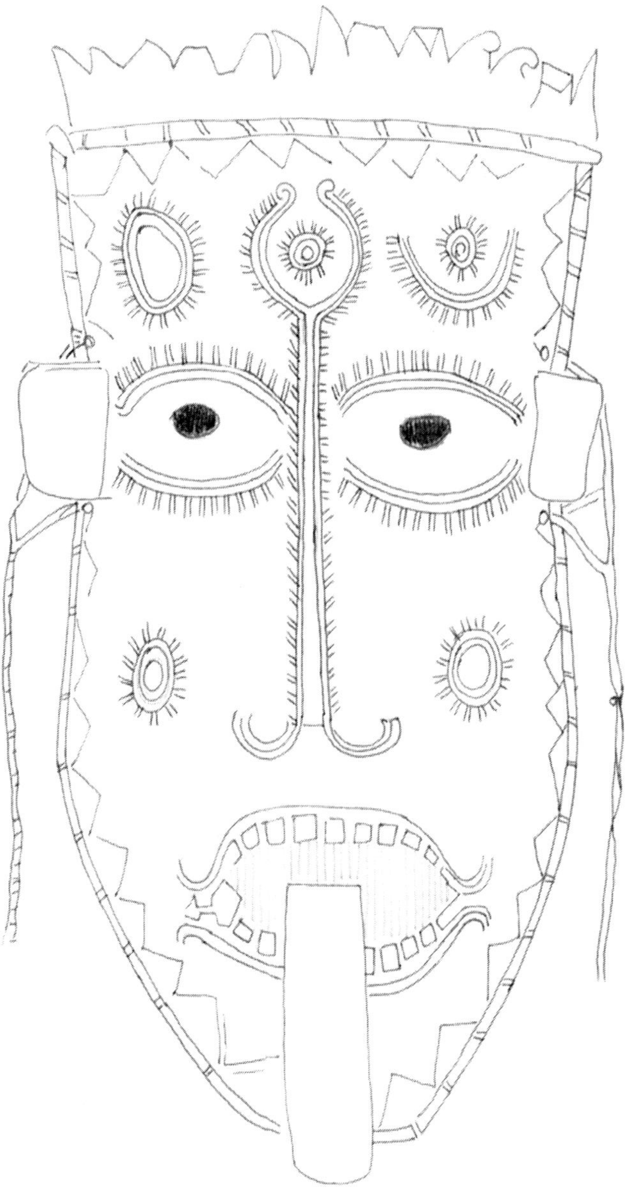

Fig. 8 : Line-drawing of Bamboo plaited mask of Goddess Kali (Char-Gog)

Fig. 9 : Photographic documentation of the Mask of Goddess Kali (Chandi) (Char-Gog)

Technology : The structural aspect of the bamboo made mask (*Char-Gog*) exhibits certain salient features. Its main constituent material is bamboo. The auxiliary items used in making the mask are cotton thread, a piece of old white cotton cloth, goat-skin and a small piece of wood (with uniform diameter all along its length). The Rabhas make use of the bamboo strips of desired size for the preparation of this mask. For the preparation of strips ideal for mask-making, they follow successive steps. For the purpose the Rabhas initially collect suitable bamboo from the near-by jungle. They next eliminate its hard basal portion and the slender upper part which are considered unsuitable for the work. They utilise the rest of the bamboo by cutting it into several pieces. Length of a piece depends upon the expected length of the mask. The length of a mask in general varies between 12 to 15 inches or so. The work for preliminary round of mask-making comes to an end at this stage.

Second phase of work starts with removal of the node, if any, at the end of each bamboo piece. The reason is that the node at the end of a piece of bamboo creates inconvenience in splitting it into several slender strips. A bamboo piece devoid of its end-nodes is first bifurcated vertically into two equal halves by making an incision at the centre. Each piece thus obtained, after bifurcation is further bifurcated. This bifurcation process goes on until the bamboo strips of desired length and breadth are obtained. Next the inner part of the strips thus obtained, are removed to minimize their thickness for making them pliable. Only the harder outer surface of the strips measuring approximately 15 inches in length, one cm. in breadth and one mm in thickness are used. Second phase of work comes to an end when the adequate number of bamboo strips required for the preparation of a mask are ready.

Third phase of work starts with the weaving of the bamboo strips by a Rabha craftsman. The basket-work undertaken in making the mask comes under the plaited category. Among the different types of plaited basket-work, the technique used in making a mask comes under the 'check' type in which the wrap and the weft pass over and under each other singly as in woven cloth. The weaving process continues till the woven part attains a size which is adequate enough for giving definite shape to a mask.

The outline of the weaved structure assumes 'U' form with the maximum breadth at the distal end. Free margin of this end is in straight line. But the proximal end takes more or less an elliptical shape. At this stage a small straight wooden piece which stands for nose is placed in the appropriate place on the weaved structure. It is firmly fixed up in place by tying it with the woven structure. A strong but slender cord is used for the purpose. Two or three shallow grooves are made at different points on the wooden piece to keep the tying cord firmly in position. The cord is made to pass over these grooves so that it may not slip at any point of time.

After the fixation of the nasal structure a piece of worn-out white cloth is tightly stretched over the entire outer surface of the weaved structure. This cloth piece is kept firmly in position by stitching it with the woven structure all along its margin. An incision is made piercing both the weaved structure and cloth-coating below the nose to make an oral opening meant for insertion of the protruded tongue. Two incisions are also made on the two lateral sides of the face at eye level for fixing up the ears. The piece of worn-out white cloth used for covering the entire outer surface of the weaved structure stands for canvas. The covering of white cloth is given for the convenience of application of colour which is not feasible directly on the rough and uneven surface of the weaved bamboo structure.

Different Stages for the preparation of bamboo strips (First stage)

Fig. 10 : Removal of end nodes

Different Stages for the preparation of bamboo strips (stage two)

Fig. 11 : Bifurcation of a piece of bamboo

Different Stages for the preparation of bamboo strips (stage three)

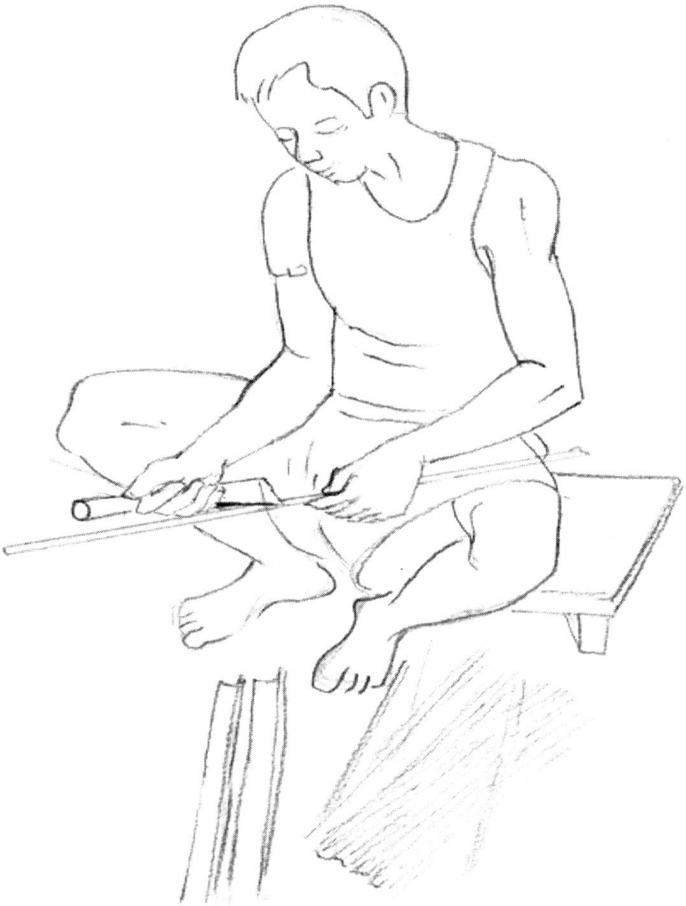

Fig. 12 : Continuation of bifurcation process (stage three)

Weaving technic of bamboo strips (stage four)

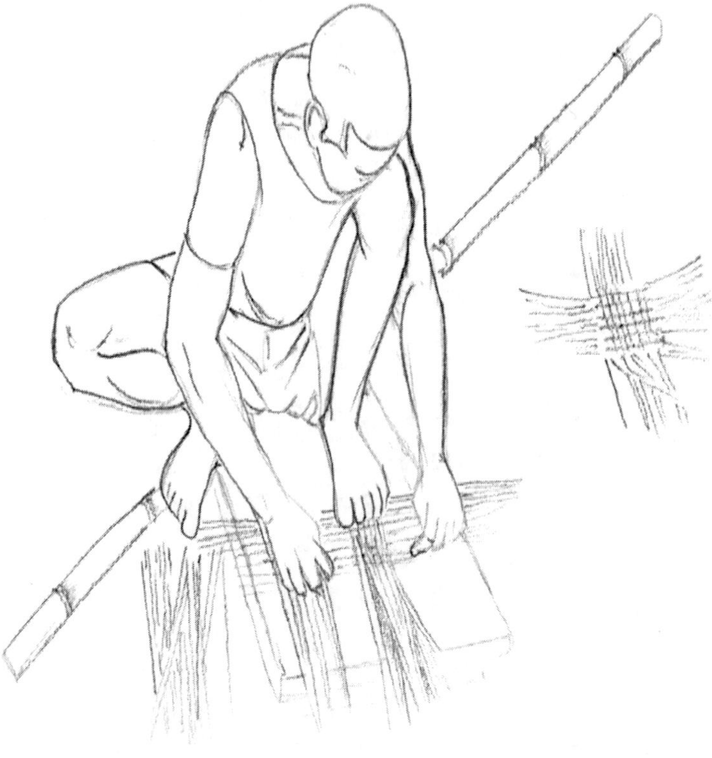

Fig. 13 : Weaving technique of bamboo strips (stage four)

Wrapping of cloth over the outer surface of the weaved structure and the painting on it are counted as special artistic work. Hence the making of mask is counted as a specialist's job. Only the Rabha craftsmen who have specialised themselves in the work usually take up the job. By no means it is open to all. Moreover it has no commercial value or financial gain. Hence the Rabhas in general do not take it up. Hardly one or two pieces of bamboo weaved mask (*Char-Gog*) are used yearly in a *bastee*. A craftsman prepares a mask free of cost to meet the social need. He feels proud by serving the society in his own way. He commands respect in the society for his voluntary service. As a token of respect the mask-maker gets a small share of the collected rice which the dancing party collects from the host *bastee*. He does not like to share this honour with any other person. Therefore, a craftsman does all the phases of work for making the mask all alone right from the collection of bamboo from the forest down to the application of finishing touches by way of painting.

To start with the painting, a coating of white colour is first applied on the surface of the cloth. Inner surface of the mask (ventral side) remains unattended. It is rough and its natural colour is retained. Lime purchased from the market is used as white colour. It is soaked in water to make the desired colour (white), which is uniformly applied all over the cloth-surface to make it ready for painting. The white colour, therefore, serves as base coating. Before the introduction of lime the Rabha craftsmen used to apply a semi-liquid paste of pounded rice (mixed with water) for the application of white colour. Apart from white, two more colours - black and red are used for painting. Lips, nasal outline, eye, eyebrow and decorative motif are depicted by way of painting. The painting is more or less an outline drawing. Black is used to draw the outline of the facial features and decorative designs. Red line is drawn parallely along the black to make the outline of the drawings more conspicuous and decorative.

The Rabha mask-makers prepare the black colour at home. They collect soot by scrapping the bottom of cooking vessels where soot is deposited in thick layers. The collected soot is mixed with mustard oil to have the desired black colour. The soot is generally collected on a banana leaf and the colour is also prepared on the same. Vermilion serves as red colour and it is purchased from the market. In the earlier days when there was no marketing opportunity the Rabha artists extracted red colour from young leaves of *Sal*, a woody plant available in good number in the forest tracts of Duars. Young leaves were pounded and the pounded leaves were squeezed to collect the juice. This extracted juice served as the red colour.

The Rabha craftsmen used brush for the application of colour. Simplest form of brush was prepared by the artists themselves out of a small piece of bamboo strip. One end of the strip was pounded for smashing. This soft smashed end of the strip served as the working end of the brush.

There is no opening for eyes on the mask. It is, therefore, difficult to draw them on the right place. There is an advantage of placing the nasal block even before stretching the white cloth over the dorsal side of the mask. The Rabha craftsmen take advantage of the predetermined placing of the nose. Taking the nasal block as index the Rabha artists draw the facial features at appropriate positions. Besides the facial features, they also draw the symbolic figures of the sun and moon on two sides of the forehead. A cup-shaped decorative design is depicted in the centre lying between the sun and the moon. A zig zag decorative, line red in colour is drawn all along the margin covering all the four sides. As the facial features are depicted by way of painting, the surface of the mask is retained absolutely flat except the region where nasal bridge is located. Therefore, there is hardly any scope for modelling and relief work on the body of the mask. Inspite of the fact the Rabha craftsmen use a bit of modelling work in depicting the protruded tongue, ears and also decorative designs along the free margin of the mask immediately above the forehead.

Modelling

The goat is the common domesticated animal of the Jungle Rabhas. Therefore, goat-skin is, readily available. It is thin and soft. Simple cutting tool is adequate enough to give desired shape by cutting it conveniently. As such, the Jungle Rabhas make use of goat-skin in presenting the protruded tongue of the mask which is one of its salient features. Besides tongue, the model of ears are fixed up at appropriate places with two pieces of goat-skin. Goat-skin is also used to decorate the free upper end of the mask. The decoration is made by a piece of goat-skin with deep serrated design at its free end. The pieces of skin used are coloured in red to bring them out conspicuously against the white background. The skins are fitted to the mask by stitching. The stitching work on the mask is done after the completion of painting.

Aesthetics

The painting which plays such an important role in giving definite appearance to the mask is done by the Rabha craftsmen themselves. But they are by far the most inexperienced in painting matter. The drawing reveals that it is the outcome of a novice hand and demonstrates very much a beginner's style and form. Considering the constituent materials, structural form, production technology, colouring materials, nature of brush, style and form of painting, it is apparent that the bamboo made mask (*Char-Gog*) of *Char-Khilainee* dance of the Jungle Rabhas is by far the most simple one and represents a typical example of traditional tribal art.

Identity

The mask depicts the angry expression through big expanded eyes, extended lips, exposed frontal teeth and protruded tongue. Piecing together all the facial features depicted on the mask, it shows that it is the mask of a female deity, Goddess *Kali* of the Hindus. But the Rabhas often mention it as the mask of Goddess *Chandi*. In Hindu religious literature Goddess *Chandi* is the synonym of Goddess *Kali* and Goddess *Durga*, deities of the *Sakta* cult.

Functional role

Mask is the central figure round which the *Char-Khilinee* dance organised. It serves as one of the channels of recreation. The mask of Goddess *Kali* among the Jungle Rabhas enjoys socio-religious importance. The spirit of the Goddess is believed to be harboured in the mask. Therefore mask was used, with its religious flavour used in revitalising the social interaction which badly needed in the forest environment during the British period. The mask with religious significance was also used by the dancing party in collecting rice and other items from the host *bastee*. Collection of rice served as an incentive among the members of the dancing party for participation in the masked dance.

2. Wooden mask

Name : Wooden mask used by the Jungle Rabhas is called *Char-Pagal* in Rabha language. Neighbouring communities did not attribute any specific name to it. It is generally referred to as Rabha wooden mask.

Locality : Rabha wooden mask is mostly confined to the Jungle Rabhas living in the forest *bastees* of the Alipurduar sub-division in district Jalpaiguri, North Bengal.

Users : Jungle Rabhas

Makers : Jungle Rabha craftsmen

Constituent materials : Wood

Size : Length varies between 10 inches and 12 inches

Breadth extends between 7 inches and 9 inches

Shape : It assumes human facial form. Lower end is elliptical in shape. The upper end is the broadest. It is straight in outline. On the whole the facial contour takes roughly the almond shape.

Body colour : White

Description : Facial contour is in the form of a common man with long face, broad forehead, deep and large eye-sockets, prominent eyes, elongated iris (painted), rectangular opening on the lower margin of the eye, prominent nasal bridge, flat cheek, elliptical shaped chin, widely open expanded lips, exposed teeth along with the suggestion of oral opening. Teeth and lips are depicted by way of painting. Among the decorative designs — figures of sun and moon are drawn on the two cheeks, one on each side. Two curved lines end in circle but in opposite direction are also drawn on the forehead for decoration. Red coloured dots are arranged in line all along the margin of both the anterior and the posterior ends. Piecing together all the facial features the mask appears to be the face of a common man but in cruder form lacking realistic touches.

Technology : The wooden mask is carved out of a block of '*Gamar*' wood. *Gamar* is a category of plant available in plenty in North Bengal. *Gamar* wood is soft and quite convenient in executing wooden sculpture. The Rabha craftsmen, therefore, select the *gamar* wood in giving definite shape to their mask which is undoubtedly an example of Rabha wood carving.

In order to give definite shape to the mask, a piece of wood is first cut to size in the form of a block or slab. The slab is next scooped out more or less uniformly making a depression which attains two to three inches in depth but leaving behind a wall hardly ½ inch in thickness all around its margin. The entire scooped side takes the form of a shallow bowl. Shallow bowl-shaped depression is made on the ventral side so that the facial features of the dancer may be comfortably accommodated in the depression without coming in contact with the hard surface of the wooden mask. After completing the work on the ventral side, the Rabha craftsmen give due attention to the modelling work on the dorsal surface. The carving work is first started on the ventral side in order to avoid any kind of damage to the facial features to be depicted on the dorsal side.

To execute the facial features on the dorsal surface, the nasal bridge is initially depicted. It is straight, elongated and maintains uniformity in breadth. The shape of the nasal bridge which is really prominent, is given by scrapping out the wood from the surrounding area.

The nasal bridge is next followed by eye-sockets. Without demarcating the nasal bridge definite position of eye-sockets cannot be spotted. The eye-sockets are two shallow roundish depressed areas located on the two sides of the nasal root. They are made by scooping out a portion of the wood from the appropriate places on the dorsal surface.

At the centre of each eye-socket there is a straight but narrow horizontally extended area made by carving. At the centre of these raised areas there are two elliptical-shaped black spots (one on each side) which stand for irises. But there is no opening in the region for viewing.

The masked dancer looks through a rectangular opening which is located in each eye-socket along its lower margin immediately below the iris. This kind of opening for viewing is the characteristic feature of the Rajbanshi mask. The Jungle Rabhas have faithfully executed it in their wooden mask which indicates that they have borrowed the conception of wooden mask from the Rajbanshis. Forehead is broad and flat offering scope for decoration through painting.

It is through painting, widely open horizontally expanded lips have been depicted. In between the two lips a horizontally extended groove is made suggesting the oral opening. Painting has also been utilised to decorate the mask. Like the *Char-Gog* (mask of Goddess *Kali*) white colour is used in *Char-Pagal* (wooden mask) as baseline coating. Similarly black and red colours are used for drawing the eyelashes demarcating the boundary of the eye-sockets. Red colour is used to earmark the lips. Both the colours are used in drawing the sun and the moon on the forehead. Both red and black colours are also used on the nasal bridge to make it visually prominent. Only red is used to decorate the forehead by line drawing.

Aesthetics

The Rabha wooden mask is one of the typical examples of the Rabha wood carving. The mask is carved out from a solid piece of wood exclusively by a Rabha craftsman. Carving appears crude in all respects. The Rabhas are very efficient in bamboo and cane-work. But

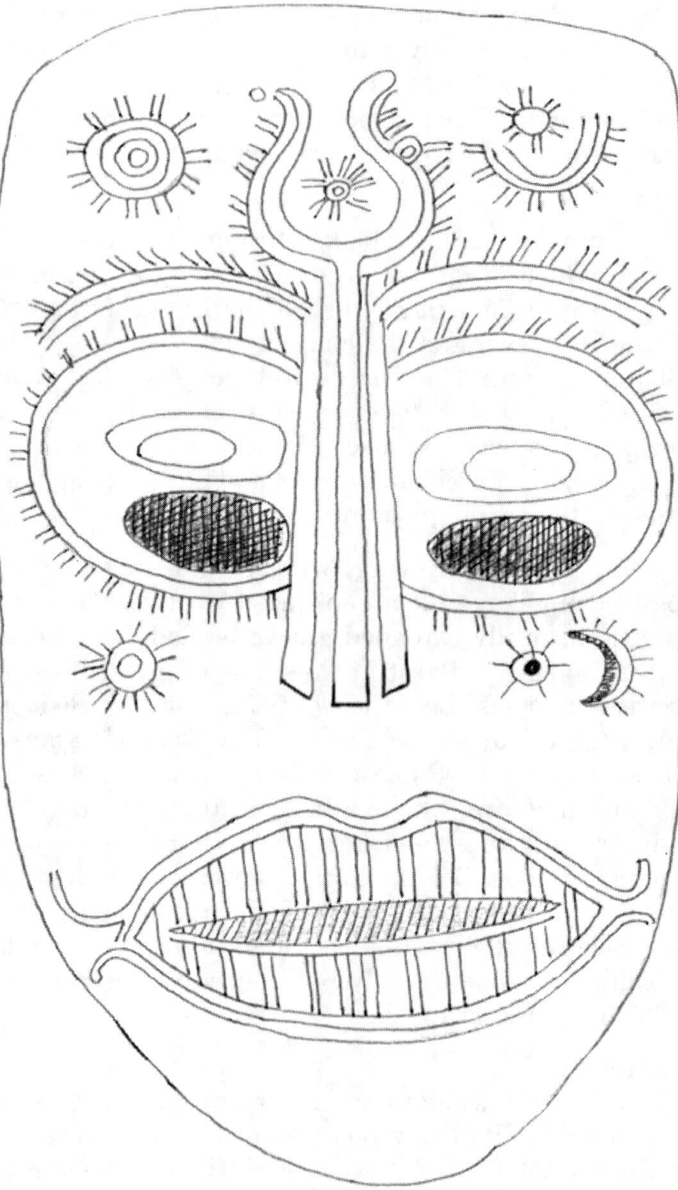

Fig. 14 : Line-drawing of a Wooden mask (Char-Pagal)

Fig. 15 : Photographic documentation of a Wooden mask (Char-Pagal)

they do not generally pay much attention towards woodwork. Besides, they do not have suitable tools both for cutting and executing carving on their woodwork. Like the bamboo and cane work the Rabha scythe (*dao*) is also the principal tool used in modelling work. This may be one of the reasons for crudeness in Rabha carving. Relief work in modelling is of poor quality. As such the mask appears to be more or less flat. Carving is traceable primarily in executing nasal bridge, slightly bulging forehead and depressed eye sockets. On the whole, finishing touch is very much wanted in Rabha wood carving as revealed from their wooden mask.

Many of the facial features like eyebrow, lip, tooth etc., are depicted on the wooden mask by way of painting. A coat of white colour is first applied all over the surface. Black colour is then used to depict the facial features. Neck to neck to each black line, parallel red line is also drawn to make the lining more conspicuous against the white background. But the drawing is very simple and plain. It is apartment that the wooden mask of the Rabhas is very simple both from technological and aesthetic points of view. With the scope of carving, drawing and painting on the same piece of mask by the tribal artists themselves, the Rabha wooden mask undoubtedly stands out prominently as an example of tribal art of the Duars region in North Bengal.

Functional role

The wooden mask (*Char-Pagal*) has no ritual significance. It is used only for entertaining the audience in the *Char-Khilainee* dance. The masked dancer entertains the onlookers by demonstrating caricature in one form or another.

3. Gourd-shell mask

Name : The gourd-shell mask in Rabha language is called '*Mapar-Char*'. From its structural features and functional role the neighbouring communities attribute its name as bear mask.

Locality : Rabha gourd-shell mask is mostly confined to the Village Rabhas living in Jalpaiguri and Coochbehar districts of North Bengal. Jungle Rabhas of Western Duars sometime use it on ceremonial occasion.

Users : Village Rabhas in particular mostly use the gourd-shell mask. Jungle Rabhas casually use it.

Makers : Mostly the Village Rabha craftsmen and occasionally the Jungle Rabha elders prepare this mask.

Constituent material : Gourd-shell.

Size : There is no specific size for the mask. It varies between 10 to 12 inches in length. Its maximum diameter at the distal end is around 20 inches or so. On the contrary diameter of the proximal end is around 18 inches.

Description : The bear-mask is tubular in form. It is a piece of elongated gourd-shell circular in diameter and open at both ends. The diameter of the mask at its distal end is bigger than the proximal end. The distal end is fixed up against the face. The mask remains in horizontal position so that the dancer can look through the circular opening which exists all along its entire length. An incision of a few inches is made at the proximal end to stand for oral opening. A coating of lime is applied on the entire outer surface of the gourd-shell. Nose, eyes and other facial features are drawn on this white surface with red and black lines. Figures of sun and moon are there on the two lateral sides of the forehead. The centre of the forehead is decorated with a small circle enclosed within two curved lines assuming the form of a cup. Short parallel lines alternatively in black and red are there for decoration all along the margin of the free distal end. Two perforations on the two lateral sides are there at this end for insertion of cord meant for tying the mask firmly with the head. There is no sign of any modelling work. All the facial features are depicted by way of painting. Structurally this is by far the simplest mask used by the Rabhas.

Technology : The bear-mask (*Char-Pagal*) is elongated in shape but circular in diameter and cylindrical in form. The Jungle Rabhas do not have desired tool for scooping out a big circular hole to give a cylindrical form to a log of wood. That is why they use gourd-shell which itself assumes a cylindrical form. The Rabhas get the supply of the required gourd-shell from their own kitchen garden. When a gourd of desired shape and size is found in the garden, it is not consumed. It is allowed to ripen on the plant. At this stage pulp, the inner content of the gourd gets dried up and shrunk. The dry pulp can conveniently be taken out leaving behind only the shell. When its inner content is removed, a spacious circular opening emerges encompassed by the shell wall. After cutting the shell at the desired points on the anterior and the posterior ends, an elongated horizontal incision is made in the narrow posterior end for demarcating it as oral opening. Structurally the mask is made ready for use only after application of white colour on the body of the mask followed by the drawing in black and red for depiction of other facial features having the same pattern as depicted in two other categories of mask.

Aesthetics : The gourd-shell mask is brittle. Therefore, there is little scope for executing modelling work on it. It is by way of painting all the facial features are depicted. As such the bear-mask does not have any aesthetics worth mentioning.

Functional role : The bear-mask itself does not have any ritual significance. This mask is largely used

Fig. 16 : Line-drawing of a gourd shell mask (Mapar-Char)

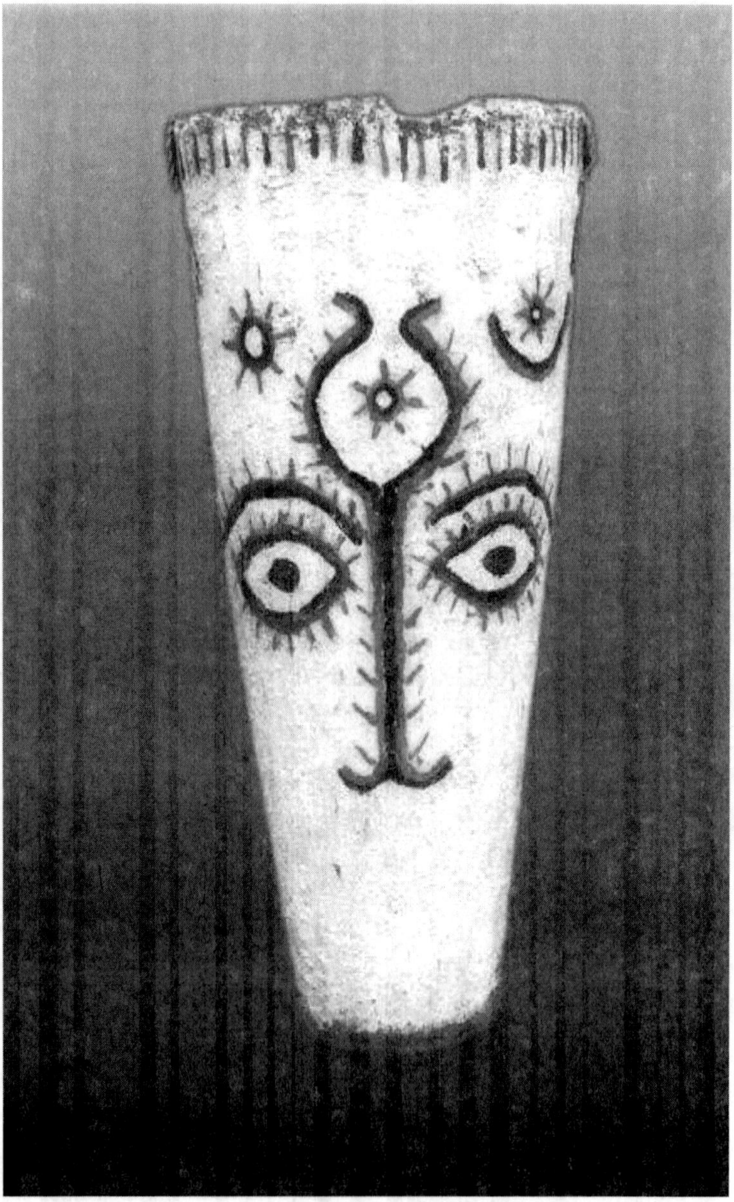

Fig. 17 : Photographic documentation of the Mask of a bear (Mapar-Char)

Fig. 18 : Mask making technology of gourd shell mask

by the Village Rabhas. It is used to make door to door collection from the Rabha villagers for organising the annual *Kali Puja* of the village. The importance of this mask is rather insignificant among the Jungle Rabhas as they do not organise any ritual activity by collecting subscription from the fellow forest *bastee* dwellers. The mask has practically no role to play in any other sphere. Casually the Jungle Rabhas prepare the bear-mask copying the Village Rabhas. As an auxiliary dancer a man with gourd-shell mask occasionally participates in the *Char-Khilainee* dance only to enhance its glamour. On the contrary, wearing bear-mask and related dress, a Village Rabha man moves from door to door followed by the musical instrument players and a batch of fellow villagers for the collection of subscription to organise the community worship of Goddess *Kali*. The party dances in the courtyard of each household in expectation of both cash and kind (rice, betel-nuts etc.) as subscription. Previously the bear was considered as one of the dangerous animals by the local people. Due attention was paid not to disturb the animal in any way. As per convention the Rabha villagers even today go out for collection of subscription along with a person in the guise of a bear with the hope that the villagers will pay their contribution generously to appease the creature (in disguise).

As the bear-mask is directly connected with the collection of subscription for the worship of Goddess *Kali*, the Village Rabhas attach a bit of religious sentiment to it. They keep the bear-mask in safe custody immediately after the collection of subscription. On the day of immersion, the bear-mask is also immersed in the river along with the earthen effigy of the Goddess.

Unlike the Village Rabhas the Jungle Rabhas do not use it with any specific end in view. They, therefore, do not attach any importance to it. Though not in use in any specific sphere they keep it in safe custody for using it at any point of time as the gourd-shell of desired size and shape meant for mask is not always readily available. Having no religious belief or ritual connection attached to it, the Jungle Rabhas simply keep it hanging on the wall of their bachelors' dormitory (*naksa*) at a safe height from the floor. Only at the time of use it is brought down and properly cleaned to make it useable at the proper place.

Salient features of Jungle Rabha masks

Jungle Rabha masks are restricted to three categories.

Each category has a specific name. The name of the Rabha masks in their own language are *Char-Gog, Char-Pagal* and *Mapar-Char*.

Constituent material of the masks differs from one another. *Char-Gog* is made of bamboo while the *Char-Pagal* is wooden. Gourd-shell is used to give definite shape to the *Mapar-Char*.

Each category of mask stands for separate character. Bamboo made mask (*Char-Gog*) represents Goddess *Kali*. Wooden mask (*Char-Pagal*) stands for a common man and gourd-shell mask (*Mapar-Char*) is the mask of an animal (bear).

Locally available materials are exclusively used in making the masks.

All the three categories of mask are prepared by the Jungle Rabha craftsmen. On the contrary, Village Rabhas prepare only the bear-mask made of gourd-shell.

The Jungle Rabhas borrowed the idea of mask from other sources but gave concrete shape to them strictly in conformity with their own conception, technological skill and aesthetic sense.

Masks reflect the technological efficiency of the Jungle Rabhas. Bamboo-strip plaited mask reveals their expertise in bamboo oriented work. On the contrary wooden mask shows their positive deficiency in wood carving. Brittle gourd-shell does not offer them any scope for application of technological skill.

Aesthetic conception of the Jungle Rabhas are manifested through painting executed on the masks.

Artistic sense of the Rabhas as revealed through painting on masks is very simple. The style and form of painting is monotonous. There is little variation in their approach as the drawing and the colour scheme of all the three categories of mask are same.

Rabha masks are the glorious examples of traditional tribal art of North Bengal.

All the Rabha masks are used in dance. But bamboo made mask of Goddess *Kali* (*Char-Gog*) enjoys socio-religious importance. On the contrary the wooden mask (*Char-Pagal*) is exclusively used for merry-making. Gourd-shell mask (*Mapar-Char*) is used by the Village Rabhas mainly for the collection of subscription from the Rabha villagers to organise the annual community worship of Goddess *Kali*. On the contrary the Jungle Rabhas occasionally use it as a ceremonial mask to add glamour to their *Char-Khilainee* dance.

5

Some Aspects of Masked Dance

Char-Khilainee is a masked dance practised by the Rabhas of West Bengal. It was practised exclusively by the Jungle Rabhas. The Jungle Rabhas (a section of the Rabhas) live in the forest *bastees* of jungle belt of Western Duars and work as forest labourers in the *Sal* plantation field managed by the State Government.

'*Char*' in Rabha language denotes 'mask'. '*Khilainee*' means 'play'. Therefore, the etymological meaning of the term *Char-Khilainee* is 'playing with mask' i.e., masked dance. It bears similarity with the name of the Rajbanshi masked dance. The Rajbanshi's have named their masked dance as *Mokha Khel* (playing with masks) which also denotes masked dance.

The Rabha masked dance which is associated with the mask of Goddess *Kali* is known by two names- *Char-Khilainee* and *Char-Kheleyee*. The Jungle Rabhas have attributed the name as *Char-Khilainee*. Occasionally it is also mentioned as *Char-Kheleyee* by others.

Nobody among the Rabhas of today knows when this dance was first introduced. They are of the opinion that it was an old practice. But the dance was prevalent among the Jungle Rabhas till the early part of 1950s. Now it is a closed chapter.

There was a specific period for organising the *Char-Khilainee* dance in a year. It could be performed on any day within the stipulated period of one month (30 days) from the date of its commencement. If the dance was performed beyond the limited period, it did not enjoy any social sanction. Date of commencement of the dance was specific. It started from the very day when the Hindus perform the worship of Goddess *Kali* (*Kali puja*) as per their yearly almanac. The date of performing *Kali puja* varies from year to year. But this variation definitely ranges between the months of October and November. Therefore, the *Char-Khilainee* dance was organised during the autumn months.

So far as timing is concerned, the masked dance was generally performed in the afternoon (preferably late afternoon) and continued up to late evening so long visibility existed. Such timing was preferred so that the *bastee* dwellers could assemble in good number without hampering their day-to-day normal economic activities. Besides, day temperature also comes down in the afternoon helping the dancers to continue their performance for longer duration. Moreover, the Jungle Rabhas had no scope for arranging artificial illumination. Dance performance, therefore, used to come to an end with the approach of darkness. The dancers, and *bastee* dwellers indulged in singing, drinking and merry-making when the pitch-darkness engulfed the area.

The dance was organised generally in a spacious courtyard preferably of the Mondal, the village headman. In absence of such a place, a suitable open space, very close to the *bastee*, was used for the purpose. The onlookers used to take their seats on the periphery of the courtyard keeping the central part completely free for the dancers. The *Char-Khilainee* dance was performed only by the male individuals. The females had nothing to do with the performance. They might be present on the occasion only as observers.

Altogether three masks - one principal mask (*Char-Gog*), the bamboo made mask of Goddess *Kali* and two other auxiliary masks (*Char-Pagal*), the wooden mask and *Mapar-Char* (gourd-shell mask) were used in *Char-Khilainee* dance. Of course, the wooden mask was introduced at a later period. Initially the bamboo made mask of Goddess *Kali* was the only mask used in the dance. Occasionally the gourd-shell mask was also used. Among these three masks, bamboo made mask was the innovation of the Jungle Rabhas. But the conception of wooden mask and the gourd-shell mask were adopted subsequently. They were adopted from the Rajbanshis and the Village Rabhas respectively.

The mask of Goddess *Kali* (*Char-Gog*) was believed to have the spiritual influence. The masked dancer with mask on, used to participate in the dance with a view to appeasing Goddess *Kali* to ensure a good harvest, a safe hunt and to ward off evils. Over and above they also did it for the well-being of the *bastee* dwellers at large. On the contrary, the dance performed by the man, wearing wooden mask (*Char-Pagal*) was meant only for merry-making. It had nothing special to do with.

The choreography of the masked dance *Char-Khilainee* was not so artistic as well as rhythmic. Dance was performed both in slow and faster speed. With sword in one hand the dancer wearing *Kali-mask*, sometime proceeded in attacking posture. Movement was then very fast. After a few minutes he fell back again and slowed down his speed while moving around. Though there was variation of speed in the execution of dance, but the choreography was in general monotonous. Being the central figure and the principal masked dancer, full attention of the assembled gathering was focussed on him. Therefore, he had to remain alert all the time in maintaining his movement whether slow or fast. It was undoubtedly a laborious process. The performance at a stretch continued at least for an hour or so. If the dancer was too much exhausted, he could sit down on the ground for taking rest to regain his strength. But it was hardly for a few minutes. During this lull period, the unmasked group dancers used to sing in louder voice and moved faster encircling the masked dancer for raising the tempo. The wooden masked dancer took this opportunity. He used to come forward from marginal area for taking up the central stage to fill up the vacancy. The wooden masked dancer tried to demonstrate his own skill when the entire attention of the assembled gathering was focussed on him. This temporary lull period used to come to an end as soon as the *Char-Gog* masked dancer got up on his feet again and started dancing as before. Choreography of the *Char-Khilainee* dance strictly confined to foot movement. Face being covered by mask and sword being firmly held by hand, there was little scope for demonstration of choreography through the movement of hands and facial expression.

Stipulated dress was there for the masked dancers. The bamboo plaited masked dancer who was the principal figure in *Char-Khilainee* dance wore a traditional colourful full sleeve female coat as the upper garment. Lower part of the body from waist to ankle was kept covered by their traditional unsewn garment — a piece of colourful cloth. He held a sword in his left hand and the right hand remained free. Being the mask of a female deity, the dancer not only wore the traditional Rabha female garments, but also used two pieces of '*Chamor*' which stand for long hair, typical of the Rabha women. '*Chamor*' is actually a tuft of black tail hair of yak fitted to a wooden handle. The handles of two '*Chamors*' were fixed up on the forehead by wrapping a cloth band around the head, thereby exposing the tuft of hair over his head. A waistband or a thick jute rope was tied around the waist of the dancer to keep both the upper and lower garments tightly in position. A long and thick band of cloth was made to pass over the shoulder in crosswise fashion for keeping the full sleeve upper garment in proper place when the dancer danced making vigorous movement. A bell was kept hanging at the back from the waistband or a thick cord serving as waistband. Not only the masked dancers, but also the ordinary dancers who participated in the dance, dressed themselves properly with their *dhoti* and shirt. They gave special attention to their head-gear. The head-gear of the Rabhas consists of a band of white cloth which is wrapped round the head in their characteristic style keeping one end hanging freely on the back.

There is a definite technique of wearing the masks. Initially a band of cloth is vertically wrapped round the head and the face of the dancer along the line of the ears taking a 'U' turn under the chin. The mask is next placed appropriately against the face resting its entire margin all along on the wrapped band of cloth without touching the facial skin anywhere. Two pieces of strong cord mostly made of jute fibres are used for fastening. One end of a cord is firmly tied to the mask on the border at eye level while its other end remains free. Similarly the another cord is also tied on the opposite side, in the same way and in the same position. The free ends of the two cords are tightly tied up at the back of the head to fix up the mask appropriately. A helping hand is required both for wrapping the cloth-band and fixing the mask by fastening the knot at the back. Fitting of the mask of Goddess *Kali* (*Char-Gog*) is a bit different. There is no opening in the eye region of the *Kali*-mask. Therefore, the mask is fitted against the face of the dancer in slanting position. Lower part of the mask is placed in a bit upward position keeping a gap between the lower part of the face and the mask so that he may see through the gap which lies between the mask and the lower part of the face.

The wooden masked dancer wore a dress of different nature. He used to wear a costume studded with jute fibres all over the body. The costume had two divisions - cotton jacket and cotton trouser meant for covering the upper and the lower parts of the body. Both the jacket and the trouser were entirely covered with tufts of jute fibre in natural colour. Each tuft of fibres was attached to the dress by stitching. A sheet of coloured cloth was used like a scarf to cover the entire head region of the dancer only exposing the face. The dancer carried a peculiar curved stick in his hand to make use of it for the sake of caricature. The mask was made to fit on the face of the dancer in the same way as was done in case of the bamboo made mask of Goddess *Kali*. But the wooden mask was provided with opening in the eye socket for looking through. Therefore, it was uniformly fitted against the face without keeping any gap between the mask and the lower part of the face of the dancer as was the case with the bamboo plaited mask (*Char-Gog*). The bamboo made mask had no opening in the eye region. Hence for the convenience of looking through the gap, the bamboo made mask was fitted with the head in slanting position.

The dress of the masked dancer using the bear-mask (made of gourd-shell), was almost like that of the wooden masked dancer. Only difference was that the colour of the tuft of jute fibres was black like the fur of the bear. The dress with cotton jacket and cotton trouser was introduced at a later period. The concept of jute fibre studded dress had been adopted from the Rajbanshis. Initially the Jungle Rabha dancers used banana leaves as dress to cover their bodies. Multiple incisions were made on the blade of the banana leaves making numerous strips which stood for hairy body.

The Jungle Rabhas used to organise the *Char-Khilainee* dance in two levels. When the dance was organised only for their own *bastee* dwellers, it was organised in smaller scale. Only the Mondal, (village headman), Deosi (village priest) and a few responsible *bastee* elders took the initiative in organising the dance. Such function was organised only once in a year. The *bastee* level dance was organised only when the *bastee* elders had no intention of visiting any neighbouring *bastee*. It was meant for merry-making only. But elaborate arrangement was needed when the dancing party of a *bastee* used to visit the neighbouring *bastee* to demonstrate their performance not only for merry-making, but also for entering into social interaction with a view to developing better social integration. But the choreography of the dance was the same whether it was organised within the *bastee* or outside.

While organising the *Char-Khilainee* dance in small scale exclusively in presence of their own *bastee* dwellers, the dancers used to start dancing in the courtyard of the Mondal at the opportune moment as per the previous arrangement. The onlookers took their seat at the periphery of the courtyard keeping the central part completely free for dance performance. The masked dancer used to dance freely in the centre. Surrounding the masked dancer other participants (musical instrument players and singers) took their position in a circle. The wooden masked dancer who actually played the role of caricaturist used to dance in the outer circle lying between the rings of musical instrument players and the onlookers. The dancing ground was, thus, divided into three circles so that the performers could perform their respective role freely without disturbing others in the process. The dancer with bamboo mask was the principle figure in the *Char-Khilainee* dance. He was, therefore, allowed to dance freely in the centre. For the purpose he was protected by the circle created by the musical instrument players and the singers. The role of the wooden masked dancer was to entertain the onlookers by his gesture and posture. Hence he used to dance in the outer circle at the close proximity to the onlookers. If he was allowed to dance in the centre, his caricature would not be clearly visible to the onlookers through the crowded legs of other performers. The very purpose of introducing the wooden masked dance would have been wasted in the process. At the time of dancing in accompaniment with the musical instruments, the singers also joined in dancing. They danced following a monotonous rhythm and moving around in a circle. The dancing session continued for more than an hour or so till the visibility became obscure. The performers then retired from dancing and indulged in drinking and other merry-making activities. Others present in the dancing ground also participated in merry-making converting it to a collective rejoicing. Each family of the *bastee* contributed some quantity of drink (prepared in respective household) for meeting the need of the occasion.

The traditional musical instruments which were integrally associated with the *Char-Khilainee* dance were bamboo flute (*Badung Duppa*), double membraned drum (*Ham*), metallic vessel (*Dabdi*) and gong (metallic percussion instrument). But *'Kal Bansi'*, a typical musical instrument (wind variety) of the Rabhas was not in use in the masked dance.

Besides singing, there were three other categories of recreational activities in *Char-Khilainee* dance. They were vigorous masked dance, monotonous group dance and caricaturable dance — all leading to recreational syndrome. Hence, the large scale attendance in the *Char-Khilainee* dance among the Jungle Rabhas was spontaneous.

Outwardly the dance was meant for merry-making. But it had other functional roles as well. The sociological analysis of the dance reveals that it played positive role in rejuvenating the social interaction among the members of the different forest *bastees*. Religious ideas associated with *Kali*-mask stood for safeguarding the dancers in their mission to visit the neighbouring *bastees*. Over and above this masked dance was believed to be a medium for appeasing Goddess *Kali* for the well-being of the community. Therefore, the *Char-Khilainee* dance was counted as a socio-religious event in the cultural life of the Jungle Rabhas.

The *Char-Khilainee* dance when organised strictly confining to the *bastee* of the organisers (intra-*bastee*), it was considered as a minor affair. It was organised in small scale primarily to indulge in merry-making within the bastee. It did not enjoy any sociological importance. But the event was taken up with much seriousness both from organisational and socio-religious point of view when the dancing party of a *bastee* used to visit the neighbouring *bastee* (intra-*bastee*) on reciprocal basis. Organisational efficiency and socio-religious import played most effective role in making the inter-*bastee* communication through the dance. Therefore, the *Char-Khilainee* dance organised by a *bastee* to visit another neighbouring *bastee* was more elaborate and functionally more potential to serve the goal for which it was introduced. Hence, the study of the sociology of the dance is very much essential to understand its relative importance in the cultural life of the Jungle Rabhas.

The Jungle Rabhas used wooden mask and gourd-shell mask mostly in the *Char-Khilainee* dance organised in small scale. Such small scale organised dance is exclusively an intra-*bastee* affair. This intra-*bastee Char-Khilainee* dance was performed almost exclusively for deriving enjoyment. Hence the wooden mask was mostly used in this dance. Gourd-shell mask (bear-mask) was also used in the intra-*bastee* masked dance for making door to door collection of drink, an essential item for merry-making on the occasion. But these two auxiliary masks practically had little role to play in the large scale and organised inter-*bastee Char-Khilainee* dance of the Jungle Rabhas.

Fig. 19 : Dancers are ready for performing dance

Fig. 20 : Dancers are in dancing mood

Fig. 21 : Costume of the Kali masked dancer (front view)

Fig. 22 : Costume of the Kali masked dancer (backside view)

Fig. 23 : Head gear of the common Rabha dancer

Fig. 24 : Preparatory stage for putting up the mask

Fig. 25 : "Chamar" - a tuft of black tail hair of Yak fitted to a wooden handle

Fig. 26 : Fitting of Chamars in the forehead region

Fig. 27 : Position of mask of Goddess Kali on the face of the dancer

Fig. 28 : Costume of the wooden masked dancer (Front view)

Fig. 29 : Costume of the wooden masked dancer (backside view)

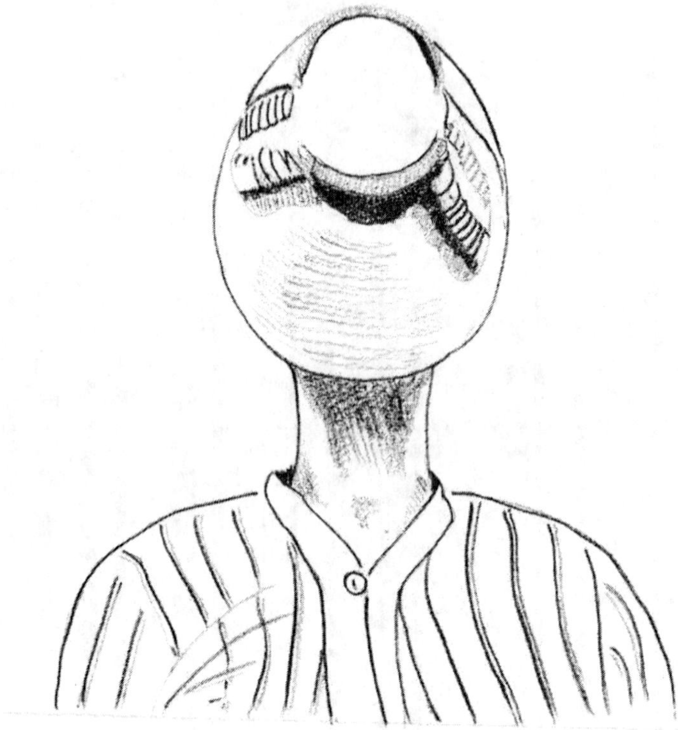

Fig. 30 : Gourd-shell mask (bear mask) fitted against the face of the dancer

Fig. 31 : Peculiar curved stick used by the Jungle Rabha dancer for performing caricature

Rabha drum

Rabha gong

Fig. 32 : Rabha musical instruments used in accompaniment with dance and vocal music

Fig. 33 : Ordinary Rabha dancers performing dance and vocal music surrounding the masked dancers

6

Organisation and Performance of Masked Dance

Organised *Char-Khilainee* dance linking neighbouring *bastees*

The *Char-Khilainee* dance organised in a *bastee* level (intra-*bastee*) had nothing to do with the concept for which it was introduced. Actually the organisational procedure and the functional role of the dance were clearly witnessed only when it had acted as a medium of communication among the neighbouring *bastees*. Hence the dance intended for inter-*bastee* communication was more well organised, functionally more potential and offered adequate scope for free mixing with the members of the host-*bastee* through its recreational activities. Arrangements made on the occasion were more elaborate and thought provoking. Procedural steps taken for successful implementation of the programme was well laid out with the primary intention of developing friendly relation among the members of the neighbouring *bastees*.

Plans and programmes

Systematic planning was necessary to undertake an organised goodwill visit to the neighbouring *bastees*. For this purpose, the *bastee* elders headed by the *Mondal* and the *Deosi* (priest) initially used to discuss among themselves about the possibility of undertaking the prospective annual visits to the neighbouring *bastees*. They used to select the name of the *bastees* to be visited and tentatively fix up the date of the proposed visits. A few days before the stipulated date they would select the members of the party and also take other preparatory steps for launching the programmes. Hence the programming of the inter-*bastee* dance was a bit time consuming affair. But the time-span of visit and reciprocal visit of the goodwill trips was strictly restricted to 30 days from the stipulated date of the Hindu *Kali-Puja* (*Diwali*). As such, the initial visit was usually made within first ten days of the specific time-span leaving behind the remaining days for making reciprocal visits. The *bastee*-elders, therefore, chalked out the programme earlier so that the trips might be undertaken in time and in a systematic way.

While preparing the programme for goodwill visit, the Rabha elders gave due consideration in terms of its impact on their economy. Sufficient quantity of rice was consumed for offering food and drink to the visiting party members. At the same time each family of the host *bastee* had to give some quantity of rice to the visiting party as a token of goodwill. To restrict the use of rice within limit, the *bastee* elders used to organise not more than one or two such visits within the stipulated period of a year. At the same time, they also restricted the number of members of the party within limit. There was no compulsion of giving rice to the dancing party on the part of a *bastee* dweller if he was really poor to do so.

Composition of the party

A dancing party was composed of 15 to 20 individuals in an average. Limited number of individuals were included in the party to keep the guest entertainment expenditure within limit. A dancing party used to visit the neighbouring *bastee* as the representative of its own *bastee*. Hence the *bastee* elders in consultation with its secular head and religious head used to select the party members. Only adult males both younger and elderly individuals were included in the party judiciously. A responsible elderly person was entrusted with the responsibility of giving leadership for maintaining co-operation among the party members and also to tackle with any problem for avoiding confusion either on the way or in the visiting *bastee*. Each individual in the party had distinct role to play in addition to participation in recreational activities. The principal mask dancer who was the central figure of the party, assisted by his helper, was responsible for maintaining the sanctity of the mask. Two or three members of the party were musical instrument players. A few elderly persons were there to look after the mutual understanding among the party members. A number of young men of the party, equipped with weapons used to stand guard on the way through the forest, infested with dangerous wildlife. Thus, assigning different responsibility to different members of the party, steps were taken to plug all the possible avenues which might create problem for making successful social contact.

Selection of masked dancer

The mask of Goddess *Kali* (*Char-Gog*) was the only mask round which the entire episode was organised. Therefore, a responsible person was assigned to play the role of the masked dancer. A sturdy young man, full of vigour and energy, was believed to be the ideal person for performing this masked dance. Different persons might play the role of the masked dancer on different occasions. But a particular person on being selected, had to play the role of the masked dancer for a specific mission. The selected dancer had to observe certain bindings for attaining mental purification required for the purpose. Therefore, from the time of leaving the *bastee* till the party returned, the selected person not only danced as masked dancer but also looked after the maintenance of ritual purity of the mask. For the maintenance of ritual purity of the mask, the dancer with mask on, was debarred from speaking. He could neither eat anything nor could attend nature's call on the way. Therefore, a helping hand was needed to assist the masked dancer whenever he was in need of help. The *bastee* elders, therefore, used to select a helper at the time of selection of the dancer. The helper used to take the charge of carrying the mask for the time being on the way, if necessary.

The dancer had to go through certain ordeals. He had to carry the mask all the way from his own *bastee* to the host *bastee*. He was to return in the same way strictly maintaining the ritual bindings. He had to go on foot all the way covering atleast 10 to 15 km or so through the inconvenient and uncongenial forest path, giving singular attention to the mask which he was carrying. On reaching the destination he had to participate in the dance lasting for an hour or so. After taking rest only for a few hours at night, he had to perform again in the morning. Thereafter, taking the morning meal he was to return to his own *bastee* covering the entire distance on foot and carrying the mask all the way. Immediately after arrival the dancer with the active assistance of his helper used to cut the bamboo made mask into pieces and threw them in the running water of the river as per their conception. As such, the dancer was the principal figure in the dance performance and the recreational activities were performed centering around him. He definitely played a dominant role in the assigned mission. Therefore, he had to bear much stress and strain both physical and mental. In view of the fact the *bastee* elders used to select a healthy, sensible and responsible person to play this specific role.

Preparation for the journey

The members of the *Char-Khilainee* dancing party had been selected earlier. Hence on the stipulated date the party members used to assemble in the courtyard of the *Mondal* (headman) around 10 A.M. after taking morning meal in their respective home with an expectation of having evening meal in the host *bastee*. The Rabhas usually take two principal meals in a day — one in the morning before leaving for work and the other in the evening on their return from field. The party members attired themselves appropriately according to their respective role in the performance. As the prestige of the *bastee* depended to a great extent on the mission, *Mondal*, the *bastee* headman and *Deosi*, the village spiritual head, along with the village elders used to assemble on the spot to convey their best wishes for the successful completion of the mission and also to boost up the morale of the members of the party. Common *bastee* dwellers, irrespective of age and sex remained present on the occasion to give a hearty send off to the party members and also to enjoy the occasion.

In front of the assembled gathering the members of the party put up a short dance performance to entertain the *bastee* dwellers. It also served as stage rehearsal before launching the actual performance in the host *bastee*. The *Mondal* was meticulous in maintaining the time of departure. At the instruction of the *Mondal* the performance was made to stop in time. After taking rest for a brief period on the spot, the party left for destination so that it could reach there in the afternoon.

In course of the journey the party members had to pass through narrow pathways in the jungle. Thick undergrowth sometimes covered these narrow passages. Occasionally branches of the big trees created obstacle making the journey a difficult one. Besides, constant fear of attack from dangerous wildlife was there. The party members, therefore, used to pass through the forest path forming a line for avoiding such difficulties. Equipped with weapons a few members both in front and at the back remained in constant vigil for protection against any eventual attack. Under the surveillance of the front and the back liners, the masked dancer and the musical instrument players always remained in the middle while passing through the forest path. The front liners also carried with them a cutting tool (scythe) which they used to clear the undergrowth and the branches of the trees creating obstacles in travelling through the jungle. So it was a bit time consuming affair. The *Mondal* was, therefore, very cautious in sending the team out of the *bastee* in time.

It was the usual practice that the dancing party was to reach the host *bastee* in the afternoon. On reaching the host *bastee* in the afternoon the party could avoid the impending danger lurking on the way. Earlier arrival also offered the *Mondal* of the host *bastee* some time for making arrangement of food and lodging for the visitors. As there was no scope for artificial lighting for illuminating the dancing ground, the masked dance was to start in mellow sunlight in the afternoon continuing up to twilight so long the visibility was there. Afternoon was also ideal time of the dance when the *bastee* dwellers could free themselves from day to day work schedule and participate in merry-making without any hindrance.

The visiting party was not accepted in the *bastee* until its *Mondal* had given due recognition to it (party). So the members of the dancing party on reaching the destination used to assemble in the courtyard of the *Mondal*. The party members would wait there till his arrival. In the meantime *bastee* dwellers came to know about the arrival of the party. With the scope of participation in merry-making the *bastee* dwellers, irrespective of age and sex used to assemble in good number in the courtyard of the *Mondal*. The *Deosi* (priest), religious head of the *bastee* who was second in command in traditional tribal society was also informed. On his arrival the *Mondal* used to introduce him with the members of the party. After introduction the *Deosi* shared the responsibility with the *Mondal* to look after the hospitality of the visiting party. In the meantime the dancing party got the chance to refresh themselves after the long tiresome journey.

After a brief resting period the members of the dancing party used to start dancing in the courtyard of the *Mondal* at the opportune moment in presence of the *bastee* dwellers. The onlookers took their seat on the periphery of the courtyard keeping the central part completely free for dance performance. The principal masked dancer used to dance freely in the centre. Surrounding the masked dancer the other participants (musical instruments players and ordinary dancers) took their position in a circle. At the time of dancing in accompaniment with musical instruments, the ordinary dancers used to sing in chorus. The dancing session continued for more than a hour or so till the visibility was minimized by the approach of the twilight. The ordinary dancers danced following a slow monotonous rhythm and moving around in a circle so that the masked dancer might not be disturbed. Three-tier recreational activities were simultaneously performed in *Char-Khilainee* dance — vigorous masked dance in the centre, lighter group dance in the middle and caricaturable dance in the outer side, followed by chorus song - all leading to recreational activities. Hence, the attendance in the *Char-Khilainee* dance was spontaneous. The male members of the host-*bastee* could participate in the dance and lend their voice in chorus along with the visiting members making it a venue of enjoyment free for all. The dance was made to stop as soon as the darkness had engulfed the *bastee*. The visiting dancers now got an opportunity to take some rest in the courtyard of the *Mondal*.

It was the responsibility of the *Mondal* to take the party to individual household for introducing the visitors with the respective head of the family of the *bastee*. The *Mondal* took the opportunity of this lull period. He along with the members of the visiting party used to perform this obligatory task. The head of the respective family felt elated as the visitors paid due respect to him by paying a visit to his house. He greeted the visitors by offering some quantity of country-liquor as a token of goodwill. If any household was left out in the process, its head of the family took it seriously and counted it as an insult. Therefore, the *Mondal* was very much cautious while taking the party from door to door. When all the families used to offer some quantity of liquor, substantial quantity of home-made drink (*Chakat*) was collected by making such a visit. After paying visit to all the families the party members along with the *Mondal* used to come back to *Mondal*'s courtyard along with the collected liquor. With the end of this introduction and collection trip the function of the mask was over for the night. The masked dancer at this stage put off his mask and kept it on a piece of wooden platform cleaned earlier. The mask along with this wooden platform was again placed on a specific place earmarked beforehand for maintaining its safety and sanctity.

It was a common custom among the Jungle Rabhas that each family of the *bastee* would take the responsibility of feeding one member of the visiting party. Two meals - one evening and one morning, were to be served. If the visitors were more in number than the number of Rabha household in the *bastee*, it was the responsibility of the *Mondal* to arrange food for the excess visitors in his own household.

After taking their meals with different families the visiting party members reassembled again in the *Mondal*'s courtyard. Within a short span of time they started dancing and singing once again. Masked dance was strictly avoided in this post-dinner session as it was exclusively meant for drinking and merry-making. Elders and youths of the host *bastee* also joined with the visiting party in group dance and lent their voice in the chorus. The drink collected earlier from the *bastee* dwellers was served freely among the participants both insiders and outsiders on the occasion. The process of merry-making in a group used to continue for sometime. At the end the *Mondal* had to make sleeping arrangement of the guests for the night. The sleeping arrangement was usually made in the bachelors' dormitory (*Naksha*).

After getting up from sleep in the morning, the visitors used to assemble in the courtyard of the *Mondal*. The masked dancer also put on the mask. They started dancing again in the *Mondal*'s house for a short while. They next met the *Deosi* in his household. Along with him and the *Mondal* the visiting party used to visit every Rabha household of the *bastee* as they did in the last evening, but this time for bidding farewell. On this occasion also each family spontaneously made presentation of country-liquor, rice, betel nut and also cash to the visiting party as the token of friendship. After meeting all the families in the *bastee* and collecting the presentations they made, the party members came back to the *Mondal*'s courtyard once again. In the meantime *bastee* male individuals both old and young also assembled there and met the party members to exchange greetings. They shared among themselves the collected liquor and drank to their hearts content. But rest of the materials received as gift were kept separately to bring them back to the own *bastee* of the visitors. In this joint session they cut jokes among themselves and indulged in other forms of merry-making. These get-together activities shortly came to an end.

After completing the morning phase of recreational activities, each member of the party used to visit the respective household stipulated last evening for his morning meal. After taking their morning meal all the members reassembled in *Mondal*'s place. The entire morning function was usually completed by around 10 A.M. The *Mondal* was very much strict in maintaining this time schedule. He made it a point that overstay of the guests might not spoil the daily economic activities of the *bastee* dwellers. At the same time the members of the visiting party could reach back to their own *bastee* in time without getting into any problem on the way due to delay in departure.

The party might visit one or more *bastees* on the way if the collection in the host *bastee* was not upto minimum expectation. Occasionally it had to cross a river in its journey. In such a case the party members worshipped the river before crossing it by offering betel-nut and betel-leaf. The idea was to seek the blessings of the supernatural power for protection from any danger on the way.

The immediate interest of the members of the party was to collect the presentation both in cash and kind from the dwellers of the host *bastee* and to participate in large scale recreational programme. Hence, the entire quantity of liquor collected from the host *bastee* was consumed there itself along with the local Rabhas as a part of recreation. Rest of the materials (both cash and kind) were brought back to their own *bastee*. In this respect the objective of both the masked dances (*Makpar Basini* of the Village Rabha and *Char-Khilainee* of the

Jungle Rabhas) was more or less same i.e. to make collection. Only difference was that the Village Rabhas utilised their bear-mask (*Char-Pagal*) to make collection from the fellow villagers for organising the annual worship of Goddess *Kali* for the welfare of the villagers. On the contrary, the collection of Jungle Rabhas made through the mask of Goddess *Kali* (*Char-Gog*) was divided among the members of the dancing party as they did not perform the worship of Goddess *Kali* in their forest environment. Therefore, on reaching their own *bastee* the party members had to undertake two responsibilities - (1) to arrange for the proper disposal of the mask and (2) to take care of the collected items till their proper distribution.

As soon as the party had reached their own *bastee*, the fellow *bastee* dwellers used to assemble in front of the *Mondal*'s house for giving them a hearty welcome for making a successful venture. In response to the welcome the party members started dancing out of joy. The fellow *bastee* dwellers also whole-heartedly used to participate in the performance making it a scene of rejoicing.

After a short dancing session the assembled gathering in a body started for the river bank to offer a ceremonial worship to the mask of Goddess *Kali* (*Char-Gog*). Immediately after the worship the mask was cut into small pieces either by the masked dancer himself or the *Deosi* (priest) and threw away all the parts into the running water of the river in order to maintain the sanctity of the mask. In this respect the Jungle Rabhas followed the Hindus, the *Rajbanshis* and the Village Rabhas who immersed the earthen image of Goddess *Kali* in water after the worship for maintaining its sanctity.

It was the responsibility of the *Mondal*, the *Deosi* and a few responsible *bastee* elders to divide the collected materials among the participating party members. But the cash money collected in the mission was not distributed among the participants. If the collected amount was good, a pig was purchased out of it. In case of small amount, dried fish was the alternative. Whether pig or dried fish, the purchased item was equally distributed among all the Rabha families of the *bastee*. In case if some amount remained in excess even after the purchase of pig or dried fish, betel-nuts were purchased out of this excess amount. These betel-nuts were then distributed among the Rabha families of the *bastee*. Apart from cash, rest of the materials collected from the host *bastee* were divided only among the members of the dancing party. In the distribution the masked dancer and the musical instrument players used to get larger share than the other participant members of the party in recognition to the special responsibility assigned to them. The mask-maker usually did not get any share. But respect was shown to him. As the craftsman prepared the mask to satisfy the social need in response to the request of the *bastee* dwellers, he did not demand any money as production cost. On the contrary the *bastee* elders on their part paid respect to him by offering a pair of betel-nut and betel leaf on the occasion. Occasionally a share from the collected rice was also given to him if the collection was good enough for distribution.

7

The Functional Role of Masked Dance

Though the migratory habit of the Rabhas ceased to exist due to forcible adoption of new occupation in *Sal* plantation field by becoming *toungya* (contract) labourers from *jhum* cultivators, yet they led their life more or less in the same traditional style as they did earlier. The Rabha forest labourers used to live in the forest environment, partially practised their traditional slash and burn method of cultivation in limited scale in *Sal* plantation field, carried out hunting, fishing and gathering economy in the forest and also followed the traditional socio-religious life. Except restriction of movement and adjustment of life style for plantation work, the tribal forest labourers used to lead somewhat the same type of social life as they did before. But restricted movement of the Jungle Rabhas gave rise to a new social problem.

Restricted movement stood in the way of making usual social contact among the members of the neighbouring forest *bastees*. The Jungle Rabhas remained preoccupied mostly with different types of seasonal economic activities. They were under constant vigil of the forest officials. Without their permission it was very difficult for the Rabha forest labourers to leave their *bastee* even for a day or so. Without completing their assigned duty nobody was permitted to go elsewhere from March to June when they remained busy with *Sal* plantation work. Besides Sal plantation work and clearing of jungle, the forest dwelling Rabhas had to take up agricultural activities in their own field allocated to them by the Forest Department. Sowing of *Aus* paddy — their principal crop, which was harvested in the month of September and October should have been completed by May. Weeding, the next phase of their agricultural operation, was continued up to June till the normal monsoon set in.

Plantation work is more or less seasonal. Working period in plantation field extends from March to June. Therefore, cultivation both in allocated agricultural field and plantation area coincides with *Sal* plantation work. As such, the Jungle Rabhas remained completely preoccupied with activities in both the spheres during this period. They had no time to deviate their attention in any other direction. So to make social contact with the fellow Rabhas of the neighbouring *bastees* during the plantation period and agricultural season in summer months (May-June) was out of question.

The summer is immediately followed by the monsoon. Monsoon in North Bengal, particularly in Duars region starts from the middle of May. Along with paddy seedlings, unwanted plants in the paddy field start growing vigorously with the approach of the early rain. Weeding is very much needed for better crop. Therefore, the Jungle Rabhas remained engrossed with weeding activities till the end of June when the monsoon starts in full swing.

Incessant rainfall during the rainy season (July-August) did not allow the Rabhas to do much outdoor work. Situation often took grievous turn when annual flood inundated the region. Occasionally the condition was further aggravated when a river changed its course. Fury of endemic diseases, malaria, kalajar, stomach ailments and other dangerous regional diseases prevailed in full force in rainy season. Emergence of leech, and injurious insects in huge number during the monsoon made life unbearable. Travel through thick undergrowth all along the narrow pathways in the forest was extremely risky when there was constant threat from poisonous snakes and dangerous wildlife. Over and above, scarcity of cereal food (paddy) at home forced them to thrive almost exclusively on jungle products. Gathering economy, therefore, took the upper hand at this juncture. Under the circumstances, natural hazards and scarcity of food primarily did not allow the Jungle Rabhas any opportunity to make a friendly visit to the neighbouring forest *bastees* during the rainy season (July-August).

Immediately after the rainy season Jungle Rabhas became seriously involved with the harvesting of *Bhadai* paddy. Its harvesting continued up to the middle of October. As the *Bhadai* paddy was so to say their life-line, they paid singular attention to this specific work. Therefore, in their new economic life as forest labourers, the Jungle Rabhas practically had no chance to visit friends and relatives living outside, for eight months in a row from March to October. This restricted movement stood in their way of making usual social contact.

Problems created in maintaining social contact, threatened social interaction. Lack of social interaction might lead to social disintegration. The Jungle Rabha elders could visualise its bad effect on Rabha society. They were, therefore, thinking in terms of introducing some measures for reviving friendly interaction among the Rabhas of the neighbouring *bastees*. They were conscious about their limited scope and tried to solve the problem within their limit and in their own way. In order to take positive step in this direction, the first and foremost problem they faced was to find out suitable time for making friendly visit to the neighbouring *bastees*.

Adequate leisure time is necessary for visit and reciprocal visit which are meant for social interaction. It was, therefore, necessary to find out right time for the purpose. From the practical point of view, the ideal period for enjoying leisure time among the Jungle Rabhas started immediately after the harvesting of the paddy in the month of October. Scope of enjoying leisure time extended up to the end of November. There was no specific type of work in the plantation field. The work in the forest was, therefore, bare minimum at this time. As such, the forest officials did not strictly enforce the rules stipulated for the forest labourers during this period. The forest labourers were very much relaxed and could undertake pleasure trip at will. As the lean period started immediately after harvesting, they possessed sufficient quantity of paddy at home for consumption. They were, therefore, in a position to entertain the guests to their liking.

The Jungle Rabhas had put up enormous labour during the summer months. They faced natural hazards and food crisis in the monsoon season. The excessive rainfall forced them to remain confined to their *bastees* and had to lead really a boring life. Severe heat of the summer months, hot and humid climate of the rainy days made their life almost unbearable. Nature starts changing with the approach of the autumn which is the regional natural phenomenon. Intensity of rainfall diminishes to a great extent. As the intensity of rainfall comes down, serpents, leech and poisonous insects mostly disappear. Severity of regional diseases appreciably comes down. Narrow pathways of the forest tracts are dried up and become congenial for movement. Unbearable hot and humid climate of the rainy season gradually dissipates. Cold breeze from the Himalayan belt starts blowing bringing the message of approaching winter. With sufficient food grains in stock and scope of enjoying leisure time at hand, the physically tired and mentally depressed Jungle Rabhas found the fresh lease of life with the approach of the autumn. They were, therefore, very much eager to participate in recreational activities.

Adequate food, drink, leisure time and favourable climate — all the essential pre-requisites at hand, the Rabha elders selected the autumn months as the ideal time for making social contact with the Rabhas of the neighbouring forest *bastees*. Such contact was primarily meant for social interaction with social integration in view. The village elders, therefore, thought in terms of organised visits and reciprocal visits so that large scale participation might take place for social interaction among the forest dwelling Rabhas. For the purpose they preferred that such organised visits might remain mostly confined to the uniethnic Jungle Rabha *bastees*. In principle it was a good move to make an opening for free mixing among the people of the neighbouring *bastees*. But there were obstacles in making its arrangement.

The Jungle Rabhas used to live in deep interior of the forest belt infested with dangerous wildlife. There was no specific road for the journey. They had to move through narrow pathways in the jungle. Travelling alone or in small number along these forest pathways was really dangerous. Night journey was strictly avoided. The Jungle Rabhas, therefore, used to move from one place to another in a batch. The *bastees* of the Rabha forest labourers were situated at some distance from one another. People could travel from one *bastee* to another only on foot. There was little scope of going to a neighbouring *bastee* and coming back to one's own in the same day after performing the programme. Overnight stay was, therefore, essential. Route march through narrow forest pathways in a batch during the day time and overnight stay in the visiting *bastee* before coming back were the usual practice for making safe journey in the forest environment. As such, the Jungle Rabha elders had to ensure not only safety and security of the visitors on the way, but also made obligatory arrangement for their food and shelter in the visiting *bastee*. For the purpose they evolved some measures and implemented them accordingly.

1. The Jungle Rabha elders meticulously planned to arrange for organised visits to the neighbouring *bastees* as a friendly gesture. Often the *Mondal*, secular headman of the *bastee* led the party giving it a special status so that it might not be neglected by the host *bastee* dwellers. In absence of the headman, a responsible person of the *bastee*, as the representative of the *Mondal* led the party. He was responsible for looking after the behaviour of the party members. He was also answerable to his *bastee* elders for any untoward incident which might take place in course of undertaking the assigned mission.

2. The visit of an organised party from a Rabha *bastee* to another was involved with the idea of boosting up the process of social interaction vis-a-vis social integration among the Jungle Rabhas. Therefore, the visit and the reciprocal visit of the organised parties remained mostly confined to the uniethnic Jungle Rabha *bastees* where the Jungle Rabhas lived in good number in compact situation.

3. It was a goodwill mission with an intention of maintaining or strengthening social integration.

Hence a well represented party was organised to make the visit effective. It was constituted with a few responsible elderly persons of the *bastee* along with a number of young individuals. To make it more representative, often it was headed by the *bastee* headman *(Mondal)*. Such an organised party of a *bastee* when made a friendly visit to a neighbouring *bastee* to renew their friendly relations, it was the responsibility of the host *bastee* to look after the well-being of the members of the visiting party. As such *Mondal*, the secular headman and *Deosi*, the religious head of the host *bastee* in co-operation with the *bastee* dwellers made all the arrangements for food, shelter and other comfort of the visitors. Alternatively, if the headman of the host *bastee* had failed to discharge his duty properly in entertaining the guests, the members of the visiting *bastee* took it as an insult which led to hostility among the dwellers of the two *bastees* jeopardising the motif of social integration. As such the *Mondal* and the elders of the host *bastee* took all the measures for the comfort of the members of the visiting party.

4. To ensure safety and comfort of the party members, the Rabha elders did not depend entirely on the mundane measures. They also tried to give supernatural coverage. For the purpose they attached a religious string to the recreational activities with a view to enforcing the members of the host *bastee* to take all the measures for the comfort of the visiting delegates for fear of incurring displeasure of the supernatural power involved in it. With this view in mind the masked dance *'Char-Khilainee'* was introduced among the Jungle Rabhas.

5. Large scale participation is necessary to carry out activities in connection with social integration. The Rabha elders showed much practical sense in this

regard. For large scale and spontaneous participation they chose a recreational device as the medium and sorted out the right time for its implementation. They rightly selected dance and music for interaction. It is through this performing art, the people of different age groups and the members of both sexes can participate freely in recreational activities without any inhibition. At the same time it is the most popular mode of recreation in the tribal world. The Rabha elders, therefore, made arrangement for organised visits and reciprocal visits of inmates of neighbouring Rabha *bastees* apparently to exchange greetings and also to pick up friendly relation through the collective participation in *Char-Khilainee* dance. The Jungle Rabhas had no opportunity of participating in any kind of recreational activity during summer and monsoon months. They were, therefore, very much keen to participate in the recreational activities which were organised in the autumn months. Hence, the Rabha elders intelligently incorporated the *Char-Khilainee* dance in the slot of the autumn months as the remedial measure for removing the mental strain of the Jungle Rabhas. As such, they instantly took up this opportunity and wholeheartedly participated in the *Char-Khilainee* dance which was one of their major recreational activities of the autumn months.

6. Double protective measures (secular and religious) were taken as full-proof measures for ensuring safety and befitting hospitality of the visiting party members in view of the dangerous environmental hazards they would have to face if they would not get proper attention in the host *bastee*.

7. Organisation of *Char-Khilainee* dance evinces the practical sense of the Rabha elders to solve their

basic problem for maintaining the status quo or strengthening social integration. They took all the possible measures which might stand in the way of successfully launching the masked dance for social interaction among the stranded members of the different forest *bastees*. Both from the climatic and the economic point of views it was the ideal time for arranging these organised recreational activities. At the same time they also took precautionary steps for safety, food, shelter and well-being of the visitors dispelling the possibility of any kind of misunderstanding in the process.

8. As the social interaction among the Jungle Rabhas of different forest *bastees* was being threatened under the then prevailing conditions, the masked dance *Char-Khilainee* which was primarily meant for strengthening social integration, remained strictly confined to the Jungle Rabhas.

In relation to the arrangement of *Char-Khilainee* dance, the Jungle Rabha elders gave due attention to the economic interest of both the hosts and the guests. *Bhadai* paddy was the principal crop of the Jungle Rabhas. The forest labourers could not produce sufficient quantity of paddy as their cultivable land was limited and production technology was poor. At the same time they did not cultivate high yielding variety of paddy. Being engaged in plantation work they did not have sufficient time to give due attention even to their limited cultivation. So their agricultural output was far from adequate.

For the greater interest of the *bastee* dwellers the Rabha elders made provision for checking the excess use of paddy, their principal crop in organising *Char-Khilainee* dance. Paddy served not only as food grain but was also used in the preparation of *chakat*, their most favourite drink. Paddy was used in the barter as well. As such, the number of participants in the visiting party was limited to minimize the expenditure. It mostly varied between 15 and 20 members. At the same time duration of their stay in the host *bastee* was also restricted. The provision was there to provide them only with two principal meals — supper on the day of arrival and morning meal in the next day, the day of departure. As such the visiting party only from the nearby *bastee* was encouraged so that it might go back to its own *bastee* within the same day. For avoiding the scope of overstaying, a party from a distant *bastee* was always discouraged. Such restriction was imposed so that the stock of food grain could not be exhausted earlier due to the excessive use of the same in uncalculative ways. At the same time for the compensation of the loss thus incurred through a visit, there was also provision of reciprocal visit. Provision of visit and reciprocal visit between the two neighbouring *bastees* for deriving enjoyment was really an ideal means adopted for interaction in the forest environment of Western Duars. A party from a *bastee* might visit another *bastee* and host *bastee* might make a reciprocal visit to the *bastee* of the visitors only once in the year and that too, within a restricted time limit.

The guests were entertained both with food and drink. Sufficient quantity of drink was provided for entertaining the guests. It was an occasion of get-together when the host *bastee* dwellers in good number also used to participate with the guests in merry-making. Hence much drink was required to satisfy both the guests and the host revellers. The Rabha drink (*chakat*) is prepared exclusively from rice. Hence sufficient quantity of rice was consumed both for food and drink during a visit. Therefore, it was really a costly affair for the host *bastee* to give befitting treatment to an organised visiting party. The Rabha elders were fully aware of the fact. In order to avoid pressure on one or two families, door to door collection was made to meet the need of the drink. The collected drink was fully consumed both by the guests and the hosts at the time of their joint revelry. Instead of making this visiting system one way traffic, they had made provision for reciprocal visit to compensate the loss of the host *bastee* thus incurred. Hence a visit was always reciprocated. As such the dwellers of the host *bastee* did not mind to give due attention to the guests in expectation of receiving similar attention and hospitality when they would make a reciprocal visit to the *bastee* of the guests. Thus a healthy interaction took place among the dwellers of different forest *bastees*.

As the mask of the *Char-Khilainee* dance symbolises the image of Goddess *Kali* (Chandi according to the Rabhas), the Jungle Rabhas organised this dance on the occasion of the worship of Goddess *Kali* as performed by the Hindus vis-a-vis the Rajbanshis and the Village Rabhas. The Jungle Rabhas did not offer any worship to the mask. They were, therefore, not concerned with the specific date of the performance. On the contrary as the mask of Goddess *Kali* among the Jungle Rabhas was used only to organise recreational activities, they did not stipulate any specific date and hour (auspicious date and time) for the performance. They rather stipulated a specific period. This period was started from the exact date of worship of Goddess *Kali* as per the Hindu almanac and was extended strictly up to 30 days from the date of commencement. This grace period of 30 days was sanctioned so that they might get some time to organise the recreational activities in the different forest *bastees* through this dance. The mask was simply utilised as a symbol of the goddess, which acted as a device for the successful implementation of the social interaction.

To control the expenditure of organising the *Char-Khilainee* dance within limit, the Jungle Rabha elders intelligently introduced certain norms.

The social norms which were introduced for successfully launching the masked dance (*Char-Khilainee*) with definite end in view, were not formulated in a day. Initially the dance was started casually. The difficulties which the Jungle Rabhas had experienced in the initial phase in organising the dance, prompted them to take effective steps for overcoming those difficulties. They took all the preventive measures out of their accumulated practical experience. In this process they combined their foresight and practical sense in admirable way. The Rabha elders strictly enforced the specific time limit for organising the *Char-Khilainee* dance. This time span was strictly stipulated to 30 days from the date of its commencement. The strict time schedule was imposed mainly to control the excess use of rice on the occasion. Instead of depending only on social obligation, they incorporated the religious belief in the dance for giving additional safeguard to the dancing party for their food and shelter in the host *bastee* under the then prevailing hostile physical environment. The host *bastee* dwellers might not give that much attention to the visitors out of only social obligation. But the addition of religious string to the mask, made it their bounden responsibility to take proper care of the guests for fear of incurring displeasure of the spirit harbouring the mask. Thereby the Rabha elders meticulously blended the social obligations with religious strings so as to achieve their goal in social front. It was through intelligence they took judicious decision capitalizing their practical experience for effectively launching the schedule of the *Char-Khilainee* dance.

The functional role of mask among the Jungle Rabhas may be divided into three categories. Association of mask with the dance had given a special status to the *Char-Khilainee* dance. Religious string was incorporated in the dance through mask for gaining whole hearted support of the community. Mask was used for making successful social interaction in the forest environment. As such, the mask in *Char-Khilainee* dance played the role as a catalytic agent in combining the three aspects of culture (social, religious and recreational) for solving their basic sociological problems arising out of local environmental condition, economic pattern and forest policy of the government. *Char-Khilainee* masked dance is, therefore, counted as a socio-religious performing art.

Like the Village Rabhas the Jungle Rabhas also utilised their mask and masked dance as the medium of collection of subscription both in cash and kind. The Village Rabhas perform '*Makpar Basini*', a masked dance (dance with bear-mask) making door to door visit for collection of rice, vegetables and also cash to organise the annual *Kali Puja* of the village. Similarly the members of the *Char-Khilainee* dance of the Jungle Rabhas also made collection visiting door to door in the host *bastee* keeping the masked dancer in the forefront. Question arises as to why the Jungle Rabhas made collection when they did not perform any organised worship of Goddess *Kali*. Here the Jungle Rabha elders showed their practical sense once again. They permitted the dancers to make collection in the host *bastee* only to distribute the collected materials among the participant members of the party. It was an incentive to the participants so that they might participate in the programme inspite of much hardship and even at the risk of their own life.

Char-Khilainee dance during the British Period

The colonial administration of North Bengal gave much importance to *Sal* plantation throughout its tenure. Forest policy introduced by the government was rigidly followed. No much deviation was made in forest policy. The forest labourers received the same treatment throughout the British Period. Their socio-economic condition remained more or less same. Regional environmental condition did not undergo much change. Condition of forest remained as before, Developmental work in the forest belt was not taken up to the desired extent. Only significant change which was observed was the introduction of tea plantation by the private owners. The conditions (environmental, economic, socio-religious, government forest policy etc.) under which the forest *bastees* were set up, remained more of less the same without undergoing any modification worth-mentioning. Hence, the *Char-Khilainee* dance which was believed to be an output of the then socio-economic condition of the Jungle Rabhas retained its functional role faithfully without undergoing any modification throughout the British period.

8

Ecology, Economy and Masked Dance of Western Duars in the Context of Space and Time

Part I : Pre-British Period

Introduction

In the earlier days the tribal people used to live more or less on their own in isolated pockets. Habitat, ecology, economy and technology played decisive role in shaping their culture pattern. With the intrusion of outsiders in the tribal belt for exploration of natural resources and also for establishing administrative control over the region, traditional tribal cultures confronted severe challenge in different fronts. In the new situation, scope of acculturation was opened up. Along with the regional ecology, economy and habitat, the forest policy of the rulers made an impact in determining the pattern of regional tribal culture. So to assess the relative position of *Char-Khilainee* dance in the cultural life of the Jungle Rabhas, forest policy of the rulers has been taken into consideration. In the then existing situation, scope of acculturation has also been dealt with. The study has been made in three time bound phases - pre-British period, British period and post-British period. In each phase the *Char-Khilainee* dance has been assessed in the context of habitat, ecology, tribal economy, government forest policy and acculturation with a view that these factors might be responsible for its introduction, propagation and extinction. So far as the space is concerned, the study has been strictly confined to the geographical areas of Western Duars in district Jalpaiguri of West Bengal.

Organised masked dance and its essential pre-requisites

The *Char-Khilainee* dance was an organised masked dance. An organised function in the cultural environment of the tribal world is generally arranged to meet their recreational, social, religious and other categories of need. Certain essential pre-requisites are there to arrange the organised social functions. Adequate financial support is needed to bear their expense. Sufficient man-power is essential for making their arrangement. Leisure time is also required for the organisers and the participants to participate in the functions. Communication facilities and social solidarity are indispensable for this purpose. Provision for food and lodging of the participants should be there for an well-organised function. Better weather condition and ideal physical environment are expected for successful arranging the outdoor organised performance. In the light of these basic essential pre-requisites, the *Char-Khilainee* dance, an organised cultural event, has been analysed in three time bound phases.

Physical features of Western Duars

The Duars region of Jalpaiguri district is a flat strip averaging about 22 miles in width. It runs along the foot of the Bhutan Hills. The basal portion of this narrow strip in the north-eastern corner of Jalpaiguri district is made up with hard stones of Miocene geological epoch. But its upper layers are covered with coarse sandy soil, boulders and gravels. Apart from the Duars region, rest part of Jalpaiguri is plain land. The surface layers of this plain land are made up with sediment.

The Riveraine character of Jalpaiguri district exhibits one of its salient topographical features. Numerous rivers and hill streams intersect the district in every direction. The slope of the Duars region in the northern part of the district is from north to south. Hence most of the rivers, particularly the big rivers (Sankosh, Raidak, Torsa, Jaldhaka, Tista and others) flow from north to south traversing almost the entire length of the district. Many of these rivers have emanated from the Bhutan Hills.

The slope of the hilly region immediately below the Bhutan Hills is really stiff with undulating surface. It serves as demarcating line between Bhutan and Jalpaiguri district. This slope is followed by gorges and valleys which are situated on the northern side of Duars. Therefore, the river water in the northern part of Jalpaiguri flows with great speed carrying rocks of different size and shape. Strong current of the rivers pushes the rocks against each other and also against hard rocks of the river-bed wearing and breaking them down. Some of the broken rocks finally get so small that they become sand. The rocks closer to the surface area in the Duars, are comparatively soft. They break down easily into sand and gravel. As a result the surface soil of the region is mostly composed with gravels (comparatively smaller in size) and coarse variety of sand. Scope of sedimentation in this region is rather remote. Surface soil of the Duars region was, therefore, infertile and unsuitable for cultivation of better varieties of paddy. On the contrary the climatic condition and the surface soil of the Western Duars were favourable for the growth of the forest. Moreover, the region was fallow, sparsely populated and undisturbed. As a result, large tracts of dense forest covered almost the entire Western Duars. Apart from the typical form of its geological formation, the Duars region is remarkable for its other physical features and environmental conditions.

Salient physical features and environmental condition of Western Duars

1. Numerous rivers and hill streams intersect Duars in every direction.
2. Inundation in Duars takes place almost in every year.
3. Occasionally a river or to change their course during flood causing serious disaster to the surrounding areas and immense misery to the local people.
4. Entire Duars region was mostly covered with dense forest.
5. Jungles of reeds, canes and heavy grass were also found growing wild in every part of the region with special reference to the river banks.
6. Forests were infested with dangerous wildlife.
7. Annual rainfall was extremely high.
8. Most unhealthy climatic condition prevailed.
9. It was a den of endemic diseases.
10. Sparsely populated tribal zone.
11. Almost complete lack of communication facilities.
12. With luxurious growth of different varieties of wood yielding plants, Duars was considered as the most valuable treasury of natural wealth in North Bengal.
13. Sufficient rain-water helped to grow deep forest not only with wood yielding plants but also with dense undergrowth full of shrubs, creepers and thick bushes.

14. The soil of the Duars region is mostly mixed with boulders, gravels, pebbles, grits, coarse sand and other kinds of material. As a result, the fertility of the soil is not up to the expectation. Being made up with porous substances, the soil does not have the capacity of retaining or holding water in the ground level making the region unsuitable for production of the better quality of crops with higher yielding capacity.

Favourable climate and environmental conditions are essential for arranging organised outdoor activities in the natural surrounding by the people of simple technology with special reference to the tribal people. The Jungle Rabhas, one of the tribes of North Bengal during the pre-British period used to live exclusively in the jungle belt of Western Duars in the midst of the wild fury of nature. The physical environment of the region at that time was, therefore, not at all congenial for leading a care-free life. The forest dwelling Rabhas had to fight constantly with hostile climate, acute regional diseases and dangerous wildlife for their existence. Apart from such hostile physical environmental conditions, the Jungle Rabhas suffered immensely for their deficiency in technology. Due to their simple technological knowledge, it was not possible for them to control nature in their favour. Instead, they tried to find out ways and means to exploit nature within the limitation of their technological knowledge. In their effort to make struggle for existence in the hostile surrounding, the Jungle Rabhas adjusted their cultural life with the local forest environment. Therefore, the natural environment of Western Duars played dominant role in regulating their traditional cultural life. As they lived in constant danger in the midst of the wild fury of nature, the Jungle Rabhas had little scope for arranging organised recreational activities in larger scale. As such, unfavourable physical and environmental conditions of Western Duars stood in their way of the Jungle Rabhas for arranging organised outdoor recreational activities during the pre-British period.

Economy of the Jungle Rabhas of Western Duars during the pre-British period

The Jungle Rabhas of Western Duars were shifting cultivators during the pre-British period. They practised slash and burn type of cultivation. The Rabhas used to practise mixed cultivation in their *jhum* field. It was through mixed cultivation, they produced both paddy and vegetables in the same field. Rice being their staple food, maximum emphasis was given on the production of paddy. *Bitirmai* (*aus*) varieties of paddy were cultivated in their *jhum* field. *Bitirmai* was cultivated in infertile high and dry land (*hatong*). Seeds of *bitirmai* varieties of paddy were usually sown in March-April and harvesting was done in August-September. As such, the autumn month was the favourite months of the Jungle Rabhas when they had stock of food grain at home. At the same time, jungle products were also utilised for consumption but mainly as supplementary items. Percentage of consumption of forest products started rising with the approach of the summer months (May-June) when the stock of food grain started diminishing in the home front. With the gradual decrease of the stock of food grain, consumption of forest products was proportionately increased to supplement the deficit.

In the rainy season (July-August) when the stock of food grain came down to bare minimum, the tribal folk of the forest belt depended almost entirely on the jungle products. They had to confront worst food crisis towards the end of the rainy season. At this critical juncture, timing for the harvesting of *bitirmai* paddy (August-

September) approached. It served as great relief to the starved forest dwellers. This was the pattern of annual economic cycle of the forest dwelling tribes in Western Duars during the pre-British period. In their mixed cultivation the Jungle Rabhas gave much emphasis on paddy for obvious reasons. Rice was their staple food. They prepared *chatak*, their most favourite drink exclusively from rice. Paddy was also used as barter to acquire articles of daily necessity from the outsiders. Paddy, therefore, served as their lifeline.

The Jungle Rabhas who practised shifting cultivation lived in the midst of forest and frequently changed the plots of their cultivable land that were enriched by a fallow. Due to infertile soil, absence of irrigation facilities and ignorance about plough and ploughing technique, the Rabhas had little scope to produce *aman*, the better variety of paddy which is mostly produced in the southern agricultural belt of the district. The tribes living in the jungle belt used to cultivate primarily the less productive coarse variety of *bitirmai* or *aus* paddy. The reasons which prompted the local tribes to pick up coarse variety of *aus* paddy as their principal crop during the pre-British period were as follows:

1. Infertile and dry *hatong* type of land in the forest belt of Western Duars was to some extent suitable only for the production of coarse varieties of *bitirmati* paddy (*aus*). The local tribal folk could not produce *aman*, the better varieties of paddy as the regional *hatong* type of land, slash and burn type of cultivation were not suitable for the cultivation of *aman* paddy. Hence the Jungle Rabhas who practised shifting cultivation in the high and dry land of Western Duars picked up the coarse *bitirmai* or *aus* paddy as their principal crop.

2. Technology of production of the coarse *bitirmai* varieties of paddy was suited to the slash and burn

type of cultivation practised by the local tribes. They were ignorant about plough and ploughing technique. Instead of plough, *bhou*, a hand operated tool was used for the preparation of soil as needed for the slash and burn type of cultivation. To suit their technology of production, the Jungle Rabhas paid almost singular attention for the cultivation of *bitir* variety of paddy, instead of *aman*, the improved variety.

3. *Hatong*, the high arable land was suitable for the production of food-crop like paddy and horticultural crops such as potato, mustard, jute, ginger, turmeric, areca nut etc. Vegetables like brinjal, chilli, pumpkin, ginger etc., were also produced along with the coarse variety of paddy (*bitirmai*) in the same field. In such mixed type of cultivation only *bitirmai*, the coarse variety of paddy could be cultivated. Hence to derive the benefit of the mixed type of cultivation the Jungle Rabhas paid specific attention for the production of coarse *bitirmai* variety of paddy in their *jhum* field during the pre-British period when they exclusively practised slash and burn cultivation.

4. The *bitirmai* varieties of paddy was harvested at a time when the Rabhas faced most difficult food crisis towards the end of rainy season (August-September). As this variety of paddy served as great relief to the local tribes at this critical juncture, the Jungle Rabhas gave special attention towards the cultivation of *bitirmai* or *aus* paddy.

From the subsistence pattern of the Jungle dwelling Rabhas it is apparent that economy of the Jungle Rabhas during the pre-British period centered round shifting cultivation, hunting and gathering. Being the principal crop derived from shifting cultivation paddy served as their life line. Their economic life, therefore, centred round the paddy. But they had to confront definite problems for the production of paddy. Soil was infertile. Production technology was primitive. Cultivation was primarily confined to the coarse variety of paddy with poor yielding capacity. These coarse varieties of paddy (*laobuchi, pauchrangpisak, sindurkuchi, jambuharas* etc.), were cultivated only once in a year (single cropping). Hence the production of paddy was very much limited. The Jungle Rabhas could hardly maintain themselves more or less half of the year with the paddy which they produced in their *jhum* field. Rest part of the year they depended mostly on hunting and gathering. Therefore, they were very much cautious in using rice at home front in day to day life. Special care was taken not to waste rice other than the genuine cause. As such, the Rabhas living in the jungle belt of Western Duars did not undertake any venture involving the use of rice for entertaining the outsiders. In absence of the scope for the production of surplus paddy, the Jungle Rabhas had no chance to undertake expenditure-prone recreational activities during the pre-British period.

Tribal life in Western Duars during the pre-British period

Before the British colonial administration took over the control of Jalpaiguri district, actually there was no positive administrative control over the forest belt of the Duars region. The tribes living in the jungle belt could, therefore, freely exploit both the forest land and the natural resources to their advantage. They led undisturbed traditional cultural life and followed a care-free life-style to suit the local ecological condition. As such, some common features in the socio-economic life of the tribes living in the Duars region of Jalpaiguri district could be traced during the pre-British period.

Common features of tribal socio-economic life

1. Majority of the local tribes were shifting cultivator.

2. They shifted from one cultivable spot to another from time to time as their shifting cultivation technique demanded.

3. The local tribes led a very primitive way of life. Their demand in life was bare minimum.

4. They depended more on hunting and gathering than on food production. Their food production capacity was far from adequate. Production technology was poor and very simple. Plough cultivation was unknown. Dibbling technique was mostly used for the sowing of paddy.

5. They were happy with the available food supply for their very existence in the then prevailing physical environment.

6. In different local administration did not make any attempt for exploitation of the forest resources during the pre-British period. The local tribes enjoyed full freedom in exploiting the forest resources and forest land.

7. The region was sparsely populated. Supply of forest products for consumption was more than adequate. Life-style and economy of the local tribes centred around the forest. Under the prevailing condition they were actually the lords of the jungle. Impact of economic freedom in their forest oriented subsistence activities was very much reflected in the socio-economic life of the regional tribes.

8. Each tribal group used to live in a specific area in order to avoid intergroup rivalry. Villages which were set up within an area were, therefore, uni-ethnic. Two tier village organisation managed by a religious head and a secular head looked after the village affairs. The village secular head was responsible for collection of tax from the villagers

on behalf of the government. Individual ownership on forest land and forest resources was denied. Collective ownership was the usual norm.

9. In their religious life the tribes living in the jungle belt were animist to the core.
10. Production and distribution were carried out through either collective or reciprocal exchange of labour.
11. Having no conflict in social, economic and religious fronts the tribes of the forest belt used to lead peaceful life during the pre-British period.
12. The tribes of Western Duars during the pre-British period almost exclusively lived in the jungle belt and strictly followed their traditional life-style. Hardly any change took place in their socio-economic and magico-religious life. There was no scope for introduction of any new cultural element from outside.

Apart from the ecological and environmental conditions, there were other factors which stood in the way of the jungle dwelling Rabhas for arranging organised socio-religious and recreational activities during the pre-British period. Adequate man-power is essential for arranging organised activities in the social context. But the Western Duars was practically unsuitable for human habitation due to its extreme unhygienic condition during the pre-British period. Severe endemic diseases, exhausting type of remittent fevers, extreme types of diarrhoea and dysentery made the life unbearable. Besides such utmost unhygienic condition, the dense forests of Western Duars were infested with dangerous wildlife. Frequent occurrence of natural hazards (excessive rainfall, innundation in monsoon months, occasional change in the course of the rivers) made the Duars region unsuitable for habitation. The region was, therefore, exclusively inhabited only by very limited number of tribal population who were the earliest inhabitants of the region. Density of population in the forest belt of Western Duars was extremely low. Dearth of man-power did not offer the forest dwelling tribes adequate scope for arranging organised socio-religious activities worth mentioning.

The forest dwelling Rabhas with limited number of population used to live scatteredly in the forest belt of Western Duars. In pursuance of their economy, they used to live in small groups. Primarily due to communication difficulties, the members of these scattered groups could not meet frequently. Scope of social communication was, therefore, limited. As such, there was little opportunity for arranging organised social and recreational activities in larger scale among the forest dwelling Rabhas.

Administrative control of the Duars belt rested either with the Bhutan rulers or the rulers of Coochbehar during the pre-British period. Rivalry between them over the occupation of Duars led to serious political unrest from time to time. Moreover, the security of property and personal safety of the people were at stake in Duars, as the Bhutanese used to attack this region frequently for plundering the local inhabitants. This political unrest did not encourage the outsiders to settle down in this desolate place. The regional rulers were also not really interested to extend their administrative influence over this sparsely populated, less productive, unhygienic and hazardous region. Due to complete absence of outsiders in the forest belt of Western Duars, there was no scope for acculturation among the jungle dwelling Rabhas of the region.

Mask of goddess *Kali* (Hindu goddess) was used in *Char-Khilainee* dance. Introduction of this mask among the Rabhas was believed to be an impact of acculturation. The Rabhas adopted this cultural element from the Hindus through the Rajbanshis. But the Rabhas living in the jungle during the pre-British period were completely cut off from the outsiders. Hence they had no scope of adopting the concept of Hindu deities in the earlier days. As such, it is believed that the masked dance (*Char-Khilainee*) was not in practice among the Jungle Rabhas during the pre-British period.

The *Char-Khilainee* was an organised masked dance. An organised group used to move from one forest *bastee* to another for its performance. They expected obligatory food and drink from the host on reciprocal basis. Therefore, it involved sufficient quantity of rice to entertain the guests. As the production of food grain (paddy) was not upto satisfaction, the forest dwelling Rabhas could not freely utilise their crops for arranging the organised expenditure-prone recreational activities like *Char-Khilainee* dance during the pre-British period.

Rabhas traditional cultural life is intimately associated with dance and music. Dance is mentioned as *basili* in Rabha language. Rabha dances are mostly performed in their social and religious functions both collectively and individually. The priest (*Sarang*) performs dance individually during the worship of Goddess *Rantuk-Basak* (family deity) and also on the occasion of *Nadaukon Bankeyee* festival. These solo dances are performed not only to appease the deity but also to execute magical performance. Dance is directly related to the funeral activities of the Rabhas. The participants in the funeral process perform dance collectively all the way to the funeral ground. Group dances are associated with their economic activities as well. *Hangai Sani* is performed on the occasion of sowing paddy. Rabha females perform group dance demonstrating the fishing technique. Their agricultural activities like reclamation of jungle covered land, preparation of soil for cultivation, sowing of seeds, weeding and harvesting are demonstrated through dance. In *Handabari*, the war dance both the sexes participate to demonstrate their heroic activities against the external enemies. Both the sections (Village Rabhas and Jungle Rabhas) do not use mask in any one of their traditional dances. Due to absence of mask in their traditional dances, it is believed that the Rabhas of the Western Duars did not use any mask in the earlier days. They had no conception about mask and did not feel the necessity of mask in any sphere of their cultural life. Therefore, it is assumed that during the pre-British period when the Rabhas of Western Duars used to lead secluded life, mask in their traditional culture was altogether absent, so also the masked dance.

To discuss the ecology and economy of Western Duars, it is apparent that extreme hostile physical environment, lack of communication facilities, inadequate man-power, dispersed settlements, infertile soil, poor production technology, cultivation of coarse variety of paddy, bare minimum production of crop and similar other factors stood in the way of the Jungle dwelling Rabhas in arranging the organised and expenditure-prone masked dance during the pre-British period.

Part II : British Period

Physical environment

The physical environment of Western Duars remained more or less same during the British period as it was in the pre-British era. Prevalence of dangerous diseases, excessive rainfall, dense forest, thick undergrowth, ferocious wild animals, poisonous snakes, injurious insects, infamous leech etc., were traced all around. As such, the local people had to face severe problems in different fronts even during the British period. With no road and communication facilities, it became all the mores difficult. Communication was by far the most serious problem of Duars both during the pre-British period and the British period. It created constraint on the social interactions among the Rabhas of the jungle belt. All these factors were not congenial for arranging outdoor organised recreational activities worth mentioning.

Administration

The Duars region of district Jalpaiguri remained out of effective control of the administrative authorities during the pre-British period. But the colonial administration established its full control over Western Duars during the British period. A forest department was set up particularly to administer the forest belt of the region. To bring it under the administrative control of the government, the entire forest belt of Western Duars was declared reserved. Having no administrative control over the forest, the forest dwelling Rabhas could freely exploit the forest products to their advantage during the pre-British period. This period was, therefore, ideal for practising their shifting cultivation and hunting-gathering economy. With the establishment of administrative control over the forest belt by the colonial power, the Rabhas lost their freedom to some extent in exploiting the forest products. The forest dwelling Rabhas used to practise slash and burn cultivation in the forest belt by clearing jungle in small pockets during the pre-British period. When the colonial administration declared the regional forests as reserved, the Rabhas lost the right of clearing jungle according to their own sweet will. The slash and burn method of cultivation as practised by them, thereby came to an end. When both shifting cultivation and hunting-gathering economy received severe jolt during the British period, the traditional economy of the Jungle Rabhas suffered a major setback.

Acculturation

According to the new forest policy of the colonial administration, the cultivators were for the first time allowed to settle in the forest belt around 1894 in connection with *taungya* (contract) sowing scheme. Initially there was no restriction on land for utilisation in cultivation under the contract sowing. In order to have the control over the cultivators, the forest department introduced some rigid restrictions in 1912. According to the new rules, an individual cultivator could not cultivate more than five acres of land. Each household could maintain only one pair of bullocks for ploughing and two milch cows. As a result of this restriction, many of the forest dwellers left the forest belt and rehabilitated themselves in the vicinity of the Rajbanshi villages situated in the fringe areas outside the forest belt. Thus the forest dwelling Rabhas for the first time came in direct contact with the outsiders (Rajbanshis) paving the way for acculturation. In the meantime, many of the forest dwelling Rabhas who could not adjust themselves to the new situation, went back to the forest to work under the forest department as per terms and conditions dictated by the administration. But a section of the Rabhas did not come back. They remained with the Rajbanshis and started a settled village life. But the communication between the settled village Rabhas and the forest dwelling Jungle Rabhas continued in the fringe areas of the forest belt for commercial interest of the forest products. Thus a channel of communication among the Rajbanshis, the village dwelling Rabhas and the Jungle Rabhas was established paving the way for acculturation. It was through this acculturation process the concept of Goddess Kali penetrated into the cultural life of the Jungle Rabhas giving rise to the concept of *Char-Khilainee* dance. There was no such scope of acculturation among the Jungle dwelling Rabhas during the pre-British period. It is believed that the scope of introduction of the dance had its root from the early part of colonial administration when the forest *bastees* in good number were set up and acculturation gained ground in these secluded and remote areas.

Cultivation

Plough cultivation brought about a revolutionary change in the economic life of the Jungle Rabhas. During the pre-British period, they could cultivate only in the infertile high and dry land (*hatang*) with the help of their very simple hand operated cultivable tool, the '*bhou*'. Land being infertile, cultivation technique only confining to dibbling and having no irrigation facilities in this category of high and dry land, the Jungle Rabhas could produce only the coarse and less productive varieties of *bitirmai* (*aus*) paddy. As such, quantitatively the production of paddy was really poor. Another reason was that they practised mixed cultivation. In the mixed cultivation paddy, the principal crop was cultivated along with a few other crops and vegetables in the same field. As a result, paddy as principal crop did not receive due attention. Moreover, single cropping was the usual practice in a calendar year. As a result, production of surplus paddy was out of question during the pre-British period. On the contrary, sufficient quantity of rice was needed for entertaining the guests in the *Char-Khilainee* dance. Therefore, the production of paddy being very much limited, question of arranging expenditure-prone organised cultural function like the *Char-Khilainee* dance did not arise during the pre-

British period. But the position was ameliorated in the British period when slash and burn method of cultivation was abolished and plough cultivation was introduced.

The forest department tried to introduce plough cultivation for the first time in the forest belt of Duars by introducing the *taungya* sowing system. It offered the local tribal population a chance to pick up the technique of plough cultivation. The forest department in the meantime banned the slash and burn cultivation for the protection of forest from random destruction. The tribes living in the forest belt had, therefore, no other alternative but to take up settled cultivation. They adopted plough and ploughing technique, an advanced cultivation device in comparison to dibbling. As such, during the first half of the British period, the forest dwelling Rabhas adopted the improved production technique which offered them scope to produce quantitatively more crop than before. The forest department also came forward to extend helping hand to the local tribes for taking up settled plough cultivation in place of their traditional slash and burn cultivations which was shifting in nature. For this purpose, each registered forest labourer was allotted five acres of land exclusively for cultivation outside the plantation field and a pair of bullocks for ploughing as an incentive to start with settled cultivation in the forest belt. Moreover, they were permitted to practise their traditional slash and burn type of cultivation in their respective allocated area in the *Sal* plantation field. With land for cultivation in hand, the tribal forest labourers grabbed the opportunity to take up the plough cultivation seriously for improving upon their production technology and its operational techniques.

During the pre-British period the Jungle Rabhas used to practise slash and burn cultivation primarily in infertile dry and high land (*hatang*) of the Western Duars. With their very simple agricultural tool (*bhou*), they could not cultivate in the more fertile low-lying wet field. But the forest department allocated all the three categories of land (high, medium high and low-lying) to the forest labourers for cultivation. Area of land allotted to the authorised labourers varied in respect of wet (plain forest) and dry (hill forest) cultivation areas. In wet cultivation areas each household was allotted with 2.5 acres of land. On the contrary in the dry cultivation areas only 1.5 acres of land were allotted to each household. With the introduction of plough for tilling, it became possible for the Jungle Rabhas to utilise both the medium high and low-lying wet field for the cultivation of paddy. But the medium high and low lying wet fields are more fertile than the dry and high land (*hatang*). Moreover, the ploughing is the better production method so far as the cultivation of paddy is concerned. With superior quality of land and production technology, scope of production of paddy was undoubtedly better during the British period in comparison to that of the pre-British era.

Taking advantage of the situation (better quality of land and improved technology of production) the jungle dwelling forest labourers started sowing seeds of the better quality of *ausdhan* in their cultivable field (medium high and low-lying wet fields) allocated to them by the forest department outside the plantation fields. Thus, at the initiative of the forest department, the sowing of two distinct varieties of *ausdhan* was started bringing desired change in cropping pattern. The traditional coarse variety of *ausdhan* (*Bhadai*) was sown in high and dry land (*hatang*) of *Sal* plantation field following the traditional slash and burn cultivation technique. On the contrary, cultivation of improved varieties of *ausdhan* was started in the medium high and low-lying wet fields using plough for the preparation of soil meant for the cultivation of these varieties of paddy. Introduction of ploughing technique brought about a revolutionary change in the cropping pattern of the jungle dwelling tribal forest labourers. Previously they could produce only one crop in a year in their cultivable land. After the introduction of plough, they could produce two varieties of paddy (*aus* and *aman*) within a year in the same field. Single cropping (*aus*) was the usual practice during the pre-British period. On the contrary, the double croppings (*aus* and *aman*) became the regular feature of cultivation during the British period. Thus, production of paddy was enhanced considerably by cultivating improved varieties of paddy in the newly acquired and more fertile medium high and low-lying wet fields by the grace of the forest department and innovative production technology by introducing plough and ploughing technique.

Timing for cultivation, particularly the sowing of the improved variety of *ausdhan*, such as *bitirpenek* or *kaldumra*, *bitirbolong*, *bitirpisak* etc., was altered marginally to accommodate the cultivation of *rawmai* or *hemtidhan* (*aman*) in the same field within the same calender year. The seeds of the coarse variety of *ausdhan* namely *laobuchi, pauchrangpisak, sindurkuchi* and *jambuharas* cultivated in the *Sal* plantation sites, were sown by dibbling in the months of March - April and were harvested in August - September. But the sowing time of the better variety of *ausdhan* cultivated in the fertile medium high and low-lying land was in February and March, a month earlier than the sowing time of the course variety of *ausdhan*. The difference between the harvesting time of both the varieties was hardly a month or so. In case of the improved variety of paddy, harvesting was undertaken from June and reached to its peak in July. But the harvesting time of the coarse variety of *bitirmai* (*ausdhan*) fluctuated between August and September. As such, production of *ausdhan* was quantitatively much more during the British period in comparison to that of the pre-British era. The Bengali month '*Bhadra*' corresponds to the English months of August - September. It starts approximately from the middle of August and extends up to the middle of September. Hence *ausdhan* harvested in the month of August-September i.e., in *Bhadra* is popularly known as *Bhadai*. Production of *aus* paddy (Bhadai) in all the three categories of land by using both the traditional (dibbling) and the advanced production technique (ploughing) during the British period, offered the scope of production of quantitatively more paddy around the autumn months. Production of excess paddy during the harvesting season of autumn months gave the Rabhas golden opportunity for arranging the expenditure-prone organised cultural activities. The next harvesting season (December-January) being at hand within the span of two months, the Rabhas courageously took the risk of using excess paddy for the recreational activities in autumn.

The succeeding session of cultivation of paddy (*hemtidhan*) was started in the same field immediately after the harvesting of *bhadai* or *ausdhan*. The second phase of cultivation was practised only in two categories of land - the medium high (*rauntaun*) and *dabal*, the low-lying arable land. Ploughing was done for the preparation of the soil. *Rawmai* or *hemitidhan* (*aman*) was exclusively cultivated in the second phase. The seeds of this category of paddy (*hemtidhan*) were sown immediately after the harvesting of *ausdhan* in the months of June-July and harvested in the months of December-January. Thus, double cropping was introduced during the British period when *bitirmai* or *ausdhan* and *rawmai* or *aman* were cultivated in the same field but in different seasons. As such, production of paddy was increased undoubtedly during the British period offering the Jungle Rabhas adequate scope for arranging the organised recreational activities like the *Char-Khilainee* dance.

During the pre-British period, cultivation was practised mostly in the infertile high and dry land (*hatang*). Coarse variety of less productive *bitirmai* or *ausdhan* was primarily cultivated. Cultivation technique was confined only to the slash and burn type. *Bhou*, the most simple hand operated tool was used for the preparation of soil. Seeds were sown by way of dibbling. No irrigation facilities were there for the production of crop in the dry and high land. Hence the production of paddy during the pre-British period was bare minimum. On the contrary all the three categories of land (*hatang, rauntaun* and *dabal*) i.e., both the fertile and the infertile categories of land were used for cultivation during the British period. Among them medium high (*rauntaun*) and low-lying wet field (*dabal*) were primarily meant for cultivation of paddy. Improved varieties of paddy and better production technique were introduced. Advanced agricultural implement (plough) was brought in for tilling the soil. Thus, production technology was improved. When the more fertile cultivable land, improved quality of seeds and advanced agricultural implement (plough) were effectively introduced, the production of crops with special reference to paddy was increased to some extent during the British period. Increase in the production of paddy offered the jungle dwelling Rabhas an opportunity to arrange organised recreational activities like the *Char-Khilainee* dance.

There are two consecutive harvesting seasons at an interval of two months. They are *autumn* (August - September) for *bitirmai* or *aus* (*bhadai*) and winter

(December - January) for *aman* or *hemtidhan*. The Rabhas suffered to the maximum extent for the scarcity of food during the rainy season. Hence they enjoyed the autumn season most when they had fresh stock of paddy at home immediately after harvesting. They used to eat and drink to their hearts' content. Timing for harvesting of *aman* paddy in winter months being at hand, the Rabhas did not hesitate even to undertake the expenditure-prone recreational activities in the autumn months. Eat, drink and be merry were the basic aim of their life at this juncture. As such, the Rabhas took up the *Char-Khilainee* dance, a time bound performance with open mind, keeping its practice strictly confined to the autumn season. Paddy was the lifeline of the organised group activities with special reference to the *Char-Khilainee* dance. The paddy was used for providing food and drink to the guests. Rice was the principal food supplied to the participants. *Chatak*, the country liquor, their one and only drink used in connection with recreational activities was exclusively prepared from rice. Besides, the rice was also liberally used as an item of gift to the guests as a token of goodwill. As such, the organisation of *Char-Khilainee* dance almost entirely depended on paddy from the economic point of view.

Apart from the incentive given to the labourers in respect of land, seeds and technology of production, the forest department also applied pressure tactics on the forest labourers so that they might take up cultivation seriously. At the same time the administrative authority took definite steps to induce the tribal forest labourers for giving serious attention to the plantation work. To achieve this objective the forest department allowed the forest labourers to practise cultivation in the *Sal* plantation field. They were also allowed to practise their traditional cultivation technique - the slash and burn method. This was undoubtedly an incentive given to the labourers for working sincerely in the plantation field. Being their traditional cultivation technique the tribal labourers practised it seriously and sincerely. By following this technique they could give equal attention both to their crops and the *Sal* saplings. Ash of the burnt jungle components (undergrowth, leaves and branches) served as manure both to the paddy seedlings and the *Sal* saplings. Weeding was also beneficial both for the rapid growth of paddy seedlings and healthy growth of *Sal* saplings. Constant watch on the plantation field was considered as an ideal device for the protection of crops and *Sal* saplings from destructive activities of the wild animals. Thus by allowing the forest labourers to cultivate in the plantation field, the forest department intelligently utilised the best possible service of the forest labourers for the cause of *Sal* saplings in one way or another. With much enthusiasm, they practised cultivation in the *Sal* plantation field where they could cultivate crops following to their traditional slash and burn technique. At the same time they could also practise mixed cultivation which they did earlier. Thus, both the forest department and the forest labourers were mutually benefited from the cultivation as practised in the plantation field.

The forest department did not make any cash payment to the forest labourers as remuneration for putting up labour in the *Sal* plantation field. Instead of cash, cultivable land outside the plantation field was allotted to each registered forest labourer in terms of '*tenants-at-will*'. That is, they would be allowed to cultivate in the allotted land so long they would be required for forest work. Moreover they were also permitted to cultivate within the plantation field, both old and new. They had no other source of income for procuring food grain (paddy). Therefore, the forest labourers put up really hard labour most sincerely to produce food grain as much as possible in their respective allocated cultivable field allotted to them by the forest department for cultivation.

Family among the labourers was well integrated and smaller in size in the earlier part of the British rule. Multiplication within a family did not take place to that extent. As such, there was little scope for division of government allocated land among the family members. A family could produce both the varieties of paddy (*aus* and *aman*) more or less in a compact piece of land. *Bhadai* paddy (*aus*) produced in plantation field and harvested in August-September was generally consumed from September to December. On the contrary, *aman* paddy was harvested in the month of *Agrahayan-Pous* (December-January). It was made use of for consumption mostly upto April. With the scarcity of cereal at home, the tribal labourers depended primarily on the exploitation of jungle products during the rainy season (July-August). Government controlled reserved forests were more or less virgin and the forest products were available in abundance. Population density in the forest was really scanty. The carrying capacity of the *jungle* was, therefore, comparatively high. Hunting - gathering economy was encouraging. As such, the forest labourers did not face much difficulty in procuring jungle products for their subsistence. At the same time they could depend on paddy produced by themselves in their own field covering more or less two-third of the year. The economic condition of the Jungle Rabhas was, therefore, much better during the British period than the pre-British era. In view of the fact, the tribal forest labourers had the courage to use a portion of their agricultural output, primarily the paddy in favour of arranging expenditure-prone organised recreational activities in larger scale but within their limit.

In order to give safeguard to the forest labourers so far as their food and shelter were concerned, the forest department took effective steps to keep control over the numerical strength of its labour force. Registration of the forest labourers was introduced for this purpose. Local forest officials kept constant vigil over the activities of the registered labourers and their family members. Therefore, there was little scope for silent intrusion of newcomers from outside. The forest officials were very much conscious in regulating the incoming of outsiders so that unchecked immigration might not jeopardise the carrying capacity of the forest land affecting the hunting-gathering economy of the registered forest labourers. Excessive exploitation of natural wealth by the registered labourers was also looked into.

The forest department not only evinced interest for *Sal* plantation but also came forward to look after the interest of the plantation labourers. Local tribal economy rested on the regional land and forest. Hence, the administration did not undertake much offensive to destabilise the regional ecological balance. At the same time the department took effective steps to keep the population density under control. Measures were taken for maintaining the status quo of the economy of the forest labourers and the forest environment. The forest labourers had, therefore, the opportunity of enjoying both the forest land and the forest products for their survival.

Scope of intrusion of immigrant labourers in the forest belt arose when the tribal folk from Chhotanagpur belt were brought to Jalpaiguri district for working in the tea gardens. At the same time the Rai, Limbu, Sherpa and others from Nepal also came down to this district for the same purpose. As the situation demanded, small fraction of these immigrant labourers tried to penetrate into the forest belt to work as forest labourers. The forest department recruited them from time to time for its labour force, but in limited number, and that too, after proper scrutiny. No separate forest *bastee* was set up for them. Their number being limited, they were made to settle in the forest *bastees* along with the local tribal labourers giving rise to multiethnic settlements. But the members of the local tribes, in general, preferred to live in a *bastee* only with the members of their own communities. Hence, uniethnic *bastees* for the local tribes were there in good number. Uniethnic forest *bastees* came into existence in the forest belt right from the early part of the British period. But the number of multiethnic *bastees* increased towards the later part of the British rule. The uniethnic forest *bastees* were comprised with a good number of families for their very existence in the hostile environment. They helped each other in all fronts, and shared both agony and joy among themselves. Co-operation and co-ordination were the basic norm of the *bastee* dwellers. Hence, the socio-cultural environment of the uniethnic forest *bastees* was ideal for arranging organised recreational activities like the *Char-Khilainee* dance.

The forest department initiated some measures both for the interest of the forest labourers and also for the betterment of the plantation work. But some of the measures taken up for plantation sometimes went against the interest of the forest labourers. Strict discipline was maintained. Rigid rules were imposed. Comfort was deliberately denied. Movement was restricted. Land for cultivation was drastically curtailed. Traditional cultivation technique (slash and burn) was banned. These measures were taken up for keeping effective control over the labourers so as to get the work done through them under duress. The labourers were not given ownership right to their allocated cultivable land. They enjoyed the land only as service *jagir* (rent free) for sustenance of their families. They could be evicted from land at any time. The forest *bastee* dwellers were considered as '*tenants-at-will*' to be allowed to stay so long as required for forest work. The forest labourers were, therefore, completely at the mercy of the forest officers.

Apart from the forest law, the forest labourers had to face restriction in different fronts. They could not change their residence independently. They were compelled to settle down in the allocated forest *bastee* to lead a sedentary life for the better interest of the plantation work. The labourers were under constant surveillance of the forest officers. They could not go out of the forest *bastee* even for a day or two without permission of the forest officials. To keep close watch on the labourers and to have regular information about their activities in day to day life, a headman (*Mondal*) was selected for each forest *bastee* from its inmates. He used to report about the activities of each labourer to the local forest officer. The labourers had, therefore, no scope of doing anything which would go against the interest of the plantation work. Provision for imposition of severe punishment was there. It was meant for discharging hard labour on the part of the forest labourers in the plantation field. They could be driven out of the *bastee* for grave indiscipline. They might be physically assaulted for dereliction of their assigned duties. Minor punishment was also imposed on them depending upon the nature of lapses. Actually the forest labourers treated like the bonded labourers.

Settlement pattern and traditional economy of the forest dwelling Rabhas were entirely changed during the British period. The type of settled life which they enjoyed during the British period was not spontaneous, but a forcible one. The forest department forcefully recruited the forest dwelling Rabhas to get the forest related work done by them. They were forced to settle down in the stipulated forest *bastees* set up for the labourers. The forest dwelling Rabhas during the British period started living in the forest *bastees* in a group. They had, therefore, adequate man-power necessary for arranging an organised event within their capacity.

Sufficient man-power, adequate financial support and better communication facilities are essential for successfully arranging an organised event. Social need is another essential pre-requisite for the purpose. In the early days, very limited number of the Rabha families used to live in small pockets in the forest environment of Western Duars. Production of food grain was rather insufficient to meet the need of entertaining the guests. It was not possible for the forest dwelling Rabhas to sponsor organised recreational activities both from the point of available man-power and production of food grain during the pre-British period. Then prevailing cultural environment, they did not even feel the necessity of arranging any organised recreational activity worth mentioning. But the picture was a bit different during the British period.

The forest dwelling Rabhas during the British period started living in the forest *bastees* in a group. They had, therefore, adequate man-power necessary for arranging an organised event within their capacity. In the forest *bastees* the Rabha labourers led a settled life. Friendly co-operation was developed among themselves for their survival in the hostile environment. It allowed them to undertake joint venture for satisfying their needs. Apart from the land allocated to them by the forest department exclusively for cultivation, the Rabha forest labourers were even allowed to cultivate food crops within the *Sal* plantation field. Moreover, they started using better varieties of paddy seeds for sowing in their cultivable field in expectation of the production of more crops. The plough was also being used for the first time to improve the technology of production. As such, they got the better opportunity for production of food grain from quantitative point of view. With these advantages at hand, the Rabha forest dwellers were in a better position to arrange organised recreational activities during the British period. One of such major organised activities, the forest dwelling Rabhas introduced for regularising social interaction through recreational activities was the *Char-Khilainee* dance.

Due to strict restriction of movement the forest *bastee* dwellers could not meet the inhabitants of the neighbouring *bastees* according to their own sweet will. The restriction of movement was so rigid that the inhabitants of a forest *bastee* could not meet with their friends and relatives living in the neighbouring *bastees* even on ceremonial occasions. In view of the imposition of rigid forest rules and prevalence of environmental hazards, the Rabhas living in the forest *bastees* drastically suffered from communication difficulties which even threatened their social integration. It became one of their burning social problems in the new situation. The Rabha elders, therefore, thought of arranging organised activities within their scope for maintaining social communication for the sake of social integration among the Rabhas living in the neighbouring forest *bastees*. One of the major organised activities the forest dwelling Rabhas introduced for social interaction was the *Char-Khilainee* dance. In response to social need it was introduced during the early part of the British rule to maintain steady social interaction among them. As the communication problem, scope of acculturation, economic condition, settlement pattern, cultural environment of the forest dwelling Rabhas and also the forest policy of the government remained more or less steady almost throughout the entire British period. The organised masked dance introduced at this time to meet the social need was practised by the Jungle Rabhas throughout the entire period of colonial administration.

Part III : Post-British Period

Change in the forest belt of Duars took place in different spheres immediately after the independence. Initially the forest department in the new situation could not so rigidly enforce the forest rules as the colonial administration did. Taking advantage of the situation during the transitional period, the forest belt of Duars came under exploitation by different categories of people threatening its ecological balance, carrying capacity of land and population density which were maintained so rigidly during the British period. The people who were interested in the forest land and forest wealth took advantage of the situation. They entered the forest belt in good number in search of their livelihood. Moreover, the then contemporary events such as the partition of Bengal and others also played definite role to bring about the process of change.

After the partition of Bengal in 1947, hundreds of tribal people from East Pakistan (now Bangladesh) migrated to West Bengal. Many of them settled down in and around the forest belt of district Jalpaiguri as the ecological condition of the region had some affinity with their homeland. By this time, many of the tea garden labourers who had come earlier from elsewhere, completed their contractual service with the tea garden managements. Some of them preferred not to continue their jobs in the tea garden any more. With sufficient vacant land available for rehabilitation, they got themselves settled down around the forest areas with the intention of exploiting both the forest land and the forest products. Density of population in and around the forest *bastees* was thereby increased.

In 1951 Indo-Nepalese treaty was signed. Taking advantage of the treaty the Nepalese in good number came down to the Duars region in search of land. With sufficient fallow land available, many of these outsiders found it rather convenient to accommodate themselves in the forest belt, particularly around the forest *bastees*. Instead of living in isolated pockets they preferred the neighbourhood of the forest *bastees* for deriving mutual help and economic co-operation from the local people.

Not to speak of the outsiders, even the family members of the registered *bastee* dwellers increased in good number by this time as they were ignorant about family planning. Moreover they had no scope of enjoying any medical facility in this regard.

Taking advantage of slackness of the forest department, the newcomers started exploiting the forest products at random for maintaining their very existence. Contractors and businessmen in good number made road in the forest belt for carrying out business of forest products. The government also encouraged the expansion of forest oriented business for earning extra revenue. As a result, large scale deforestation was in process right from the very beginning of the era of independence. It led to rapid change in the physical environment of Duars.

Due to influx of outsiders the population around the forest *bastees* was considerably increased. In some cases the outsiders in good number somehow sneaked into the *bastee* areas outnumbering labourers. The number of inhabitants in the forest *bastees* were increased to such an extent that the population density of the region sharply went up and the carrying capacity of the area was jeopardised.

Collection of forest products was one of the major subsistence activities of the registered forest labourers. With the increase of population in and around the forest *bastees*, competition for gathering forest products gained momentum. As a result the registered forest labourers had to confront with much hazards in carrying out their hunting-gathering economy. Regional ecological balance was thereby disturbed.

The money lenders took advantage of the situation. Along with other exploiters they also entered in the forest belt in good number. Innocence, simplicity and helplessness of the forest labourers prompted the exploiters to exploit them freely. It made the life of the forest labourers more miserable.

New forest policy of independent India was introduced in 1952. It imposed more stringent measures on the hunting-gathering economy of the forest dwelling tribes. The advantages which they derived during the British period for exploitation of forest products were appreciably curtailed. Hunting in the jungle was prohibited giving severe jolt to their forest oriented economy. Not only the hunting-gathering economy, but also the agricultural economy of the forest labourers was affected.

In the initial phase of the independent era, the forest department debarred the tribal labourers of the forest *bastees* from practising mixed cultivation in the *Sal* plantation field. They were then permitted only to cultivate in their allocated cultivable land (*Rauntaun* and *Dabal* types) outside the plantation field. The forest labourers used to cultivate mostly the *aman* paddy in these categories of land. Hence they partially lost the scope of cultivation of *aus* paddy (*Bhadai* type), which was considered as their principal crop during the British period.

Stoppage of cultivation in the plantation field made profound impact in the economic life of the Rabha forest labourers. *Bhadai* paddy (*bitirmai* or *ausdhan*) was mostly cultivated in the plantation field. As per their economic practices during the British period, the forest labourers used to face serious food crisis during the rainy season and in the beginning of the autumn. This variety of paddy (*Bhadai*) which was harvested in autumn months (September-October) helped them to tide over the seasonal food crisis. This paddy was profitably utilised not only for food and preparation of drink (*chatak*) but was also used in organising seasonal recreational activities and social functions. It was used in barter as well. *Char-Khilainee*, an organised masked dance of the Jungle Rabhas was performed in the autumn months, the harvesting season of *Bhadai* paddy. Paddy was needed in this organised dance for supplying food to the members of the dancing party and also for preparation of rice beer (*chatak*) — two most important items used for guest entertainment on the occasion. Moreover, each one of the host family used to give some quantity of rice to the dancing party as a token of goodwill. *Bhadai* paddy was, therefore, counted as the lifeline of the *Char-Khilainee* dance.

At the time of setting up of a forest *bastee*, land for cultivation was allocated only to the registered labourers by the forest department. Quantum of land allocated initially to a labourer was tolerably good. Landholder himself cultivated the land. Production was, therefore, encouraging. But the picture became gloomy towards the end of the British period. At this time the family members of the forest labourers were increased in number. The land of the registered households had been fragmented unofficially among the progeny of the recorded labourers. Land holding of a family thereby became small. As such, familywise production of crop had also come down appreciably. Many of the forest labourers, therefore, gradually lost interest in cultivation by themselves and resorted to share-cropping or mortgage.

The Jungle Rabhas gave up the habit of shifting habitation and started living sedentary life right from the early stage of the British rule. From this time onward they got the opportunity of producing seasonal *Bhadai* paddy (*ausdhan*) in the plantation field. The regular production of this variety of paddy in plantation field was assured till the end of the British period. Depending on this variety of paddy the Rabha forest labourers perhaps introduced *Char-Khilainee* dance not only as a means of recreation but also to meet their social need. In the initial phase of the British rule the traditional economy of the forest dwelling Rabhas underwent radical change at the instance of the forest department. This new economic pattern of the forest labourers as dictated by the forest department did not undergo any major change during the entire British period. Hence, the masked dance based on a specific type of economy, was practised by the Rabha forest labourers without any hindrance.

But the economy of the forest labourers received a rude jolt immediately after independence. The forest department took some stringent measures for the better interest of the *Sal* saplings. Much taller jute and mustard plants which also grew in the mixed cultivation along with the *Bhadai* paddy in the plantation field used to give coverage to the short height *Sal* saplings partially cutting off sun light instead of directly falling on them. It was assumed that this coverage stood in the way of vigorous growth of the *Sal* saplings. At the same time *Bhadai* paddy is one of the most favourite items of food of the elephants. Herds of elephant used to invade the plantation field in search of *Bhadai* paddy around the harvesting season. Along with paddy they also destroyed the *Sal* saplings. As such for the better interest of the *Sal* saplings, the forest department debarred the forest labourers from cultivation in the plantation field within a few years after independence.

With the abolition of cultivation in *Sal* plantation field, the Rabha forest labourers lost the scope of harvesting paddy in the early part of autumn. Their cultivation now remained confined only to wet and semi-wet land situated outside the plantation field. The forest labourers used to cultivate mostly *rawmai* / *amandhan* (*hemtidhan*) in these categories of land which they harvested in the months of December and January.

During the British period the Rabha forest labourers faced serious food crisis mostly in the rainy season (July - August). They could overcome the crisis by harvesting *Bhadai* paddy (*ausdhan*) in the later part of rainy season and in the early part of autumn. But with the abolition of cultivation in plantation field they lost the scope of getting food crops immediately after the rainy season. Thereby their crisis for food was extended upto December-January till they could harvest *amandhan* grown in *Dabal* (low) and *Rauntaun* (medium high) types of land outside the plantation field. As a result the autumn months which were counted as golden period in the economic life of the Jungle Rabhas in British period became a dark period in independent India.

The *Char-Khilainee* dance was in regular practice during the British period when the forest labourers had adequate supply of rice in the autumn months. But it came to a halt as soon as the cultivation in plantation field was stopped and scope of harvesting paddy during autumn ceased. Cessation of harvesting paddy in autumn led to disastrous consequence in their economic life. The impact of economic hardship in the early part of independence was reflected in the cultural life of the forests labourers.

The Jungle Rabhas had to struggle hard for mere survival during the autumn months in the post-independent period. Therefore, the question of organising a bit expensive recreational activity at this time did not arise. As such the forest labourers had no way out but to give up outright their expensive *Char-Khilainee* dance.

Government order was promulgated prohibiting cultivation in the plantation field in the early 1950s. Performance of the dance was stopped from that very year when the cultivation was debarred in plantation field. The cultivation of *Bhadai* paddy in plantation field was forced to stop all on a sudden by the forest department. As such this performing art which was entirely dependent on *Bhadai* paddy was also suddenly stopped offering it no scope for continuation any more.

Actually to serve their own purpose the Rabha forest labourers introduced the masked dance strictly in conformity with the regional physical environment, forest policy of the government and their own economic pattern as existed in the early phase of the British rule. But distinct change took place in all these aspects in the post-independent period. Impact of these changes was witnessed in different spheres of their cultural life. The *Char-Khilainee* dance was of no exception. Changes witnessed in the physical and the cultural environment of Duars led to the disappearance of the dance from their cultural life.

9

Epilogue

The forest belt of Western Duars is in a process of change to in different fronts since the inception of independence. Deforestation in large scale are taking place in different parts of the forest areas due to rampant unauthorised exploitation of forest and forest products. Wildlife in the jungle belt has also started diminishing along with the large scale deforestation. With extensive deforestation, rainfall in Duars region has been substantially reduced as well. With the reduction of flora, fauna and rainfall, the natural environment of Duars has been radically changed. Change in physical environment has brought about some changes in the cultural environment of the tribes of Duars. With the influx of the outsiders in good number, density of population in the Duars region has been substantially increased. With the increase of population, the carrying capacity of land around the forest *bastees* has been appreciably reduced. With the shifting of power from colonial administration to independent India, the forest policy of the government has been changed. With the change of forest policy in independent India, the hunting-gathering economy of the forest dwelling tribes has been adversely affected. With the abolition of the concession of cultivation in the *Sal* plantation field in

Duars, together with increase in density of population and fall in the carrying capacity of land, the forest dwelling Rabhas had to confront with major economic crisis. This economic crisis was by far the most vital factor in bringing about change in their cultural life. With the crisis in economic front, the Rabha forest labourers had no other alternative but to give up the practice of their *Char-Khilainee* dance, which involved much expenditure. Besides the economic aspect, the *Char-Khilainee* dance started loosing its importance when its functional role in cultural life was declining steadily right from the inception of independence. In the background of physical environment, economic pattern and forest policy of the government, the dance initially used to serve as the channel of recreation. Also served as a medium of social interaction for strengthening social integration which was so needed for the members of the isolated forest *bastees* during the British period. In the background of the discussion on the emergence, propagation and decline of the *Char-Khilainee* dance, it is equally important to consider whether there is any scope of revival of the dance under the existing circumstances. This aspect has been dealt with in this concluding chapter.

With the change of ecology, economy and government forest policy, the cultural environment of the Rabha forest labourers has undergone considerable change in independent India. The impact of these changes has been reflected in *Char-Khilainee* dance. In the new situation they do not consider any more the importance of the functional role of this masked dance in their social life. Hence, the Rabha forest labourers are not interested for its revival.

The Rabha forest *bastee* dwellers are no longer isolated. The forests rules meant for the forest labourers are not so rigidly enforced at present. They can visit friends and relatives living in the nearby *bastees* whenever they like. Menace of the dangerous wildlife does not exit any more. The forest labourers can conveniently cover longer distance without facing any hazard from the wildlife on the way. Transport and communication facilities have been improved. Roads have been laid out in different parts of the forest belt. Forest labourers can now conveniently move from one place to another in response to social call or any other need. As such, they no longer suffer from social isolation. With all these facilities, the Rabha forest labourers do not feel the absolute necessity of maintaining social communication through the organised *Char-Khilainee* dance any more. This masked dance has, therefore, lost its functional importance in their cultural life for maintaining social communication. With the abolition of the scope of cultivation of *bhadai* paddy in the plantation field during the post-British period, the Jungle Rabhas are now facing serious food crisis during the autumn months when the *Char-Khilainee* dance was performed. It is now beyond their capacity to bear the expense involved in the dance. The Rabha forest labourers are, therefore, not interested to revive the dance once again at the cost of much expenditure involve in it.

The Jungle Rabha economy of the British period suffered much since the early years of independence when the forest department debarred them to practise cultivation in the *Sal* plantation field. Their economy suffered another shock when the *taungya* system was abolished. In the *taungya* system the working population, irrespective of sex were engaged in the forest related work. With the abolition of the said system female participation in the forest oriented work simultaneously ceased to exist. When the *taungya* system was in existence the forest officials did not pay any kind of wage to the forest labourers. As compensation, each registered forest labourer received limited area of land for cultivation outside the plantation field. At the same time they were also permitted to cultivate within the plantation area. The wage system came into existence only after the abolition of *taungya* system in the early part of 1970s. In 1982 the minimum daily wage for a forest worker was fixed at Rs 8.50. Not to speak of their poor daily wage, even the forest authorities normally provide only three to four months' work to the approved workers in a year. Rest of the time they engage themselves primarily in cultivation. But the cultivation as the source of earning is also not encouraging.

The landholding of the registered forest labourers have been fragmented unofficially among their progeny. As a result, the size of the landholding of each household is now quite small. Many of the forest labourers have, therefore, lost interest in cultivation. They have either mortgaged their land and turned into landless farmers or have entered into agreement with the share-croppers. Three types of farmers - landless, marginal and small are now there among the Jungle Rabhas. Medium and big farmers are altogether absent. There are four agrarian categories found among them such as non-cultivating owners, self-cultivators, share-croppers and agricultural labourers. Till now the economy of the Jungle Rabhas depends on cultivation and forest products. With the abolition of cultivation in the *Sal* plantation field and fragmentation of government allocated cultivable land, the cultivation among the Jungle Rabhas does not hold good any more. To tackle the problem of economic hardship a few members of the Rabha younger generations living in the forest *bastees* are indulging in criminal activities. They are helping the wood-smugglers to smuggle wood from the forest.

Police reports also reveal that the Jungle Rabhas now-a-days occasionally participate in the highway rubbery in the jungle belt. As such, with the sharp decline of economic condition in the post-independent period, the Jungle Rabhas are not at all interested to revive their expenditure-prone *Char-Khilainee* dance any more.

Concept of the dance is associated with the Hindu goddess *Kali*. It was, therefore, organised in autumn months around the time of worship of the Goddess. There is no scope of shifting the timing of the dance in December - January (winter months) when *aman* paddy is harvested and the Rabha forest labourers are in a position to bear the expenditure involved in the dance. Religious value attached with the dance does not allow the Jungle Rabhas to change the scheduled timing of organising the dance. So it is difficult to revive the dance according to their convenience.

The full-fledged *Char-Khilainee* dance is not in practice for over a period of five decades or so. Majority of the dancers who actually organised and participated in the dance are no more. Those who are still alive are very small in number. They are too old to give the leadership. Even in earlier days hardly a few among the forest dwelling Rabhas could prepare the masks. Most of them belong to the members of the older generations. All these craftsmen are now dead. As the dance is not in practice since early 1950s, the younger generations of the Jungle Rabhas have not even seen the dance in their life-time. They have, therefore, no idea about the dance and the art of mask-making. When the younger generations are fully ignorant both about the masks and the masked dance the forest dwelling Rabhas, particularly the younger generations have little interest to revive this performing art once again.

The Rabha forest labourers performed the *Char-Khilainee* dance regularly till early 1950s. Since then, no attempt has so far been made in any forest *bastee* to organise the full-fledged dance as per the Rabha customary norms. At times the dance was organised in a *bastee* casually once or twice for the sake of demonstration at the instance of the local non-tribal cultural organisations. But it has lost its social significance. The *Char-Khilianee* dance is now considered as an obsolete performing art. There is hardly any scope of revival of the dance in the context of contemporary ecology of Duars and economy of the forest dwelling Rabhas. The existing government forest policy has also contributed its part in the obliteration of this particular cultural item from the life of the tribe under study.

But there is a remote chance of reviving the dance, rather in superficial manner. Local non-tribal cultural organizations, cultural divisions of the State Government and the Central Government are now trying to revive the vanishing tribal performing arts. They are encouraging the educated tribal youths to take the leadership in this sphere. Nehru Yuvak Kendra of Alipurduar took interest for revival of the *Char-Khilainee* dance in 1980s. Under the banner of the tribal cultural organisations this dance could be patronised for revival as an item of performing art only for demonstration in the different regional cultural functions unrelated with the traditional socio-religious life of the Jungle Rabhas.

In the context of the traditional anthropological research, this brief report has been placed as the culture history of a tribal community over a chosen time frame. This specific cultural item in terms of its continuity and change has been narrated with a special emphasis.

Though this may not be generalised, but not withstanding the limitations, the present observations may be hopefully compared with the similar instances in any part of the country.

The publication deserves attention as a museum publication for highlighting the databased ethnographic objects. The data utilised in this publication were collected in connection with the collection of anthropological specimens for enriching the ethnographic collection of the Indian Museum. The specimens are the backbone of a museum. The relative importance of a museum again depends upon its collection. As such, the collection of ethnographic specimens is by far one of the major baseline work of an ethnographic museum. The anthropology section of the Indian Museum, therefore, took up an extensive field work in 1981 and 1982 for making the collection of traditional cultural artifacts (ethnographic objects) of the Jungle Rabhas of North Bengal to build up the collection of the Indian Museum from that region.

The traditional cultural artifacts of the tribal and folk cultures are in a process of rapid change. In the changing situation many of the traditional cultural artifacts of the people of simple technology have already become extinct by now and some are on the verge of extinction. Hence it is the bounden responsibility of the ethnographic museums to collect and preserve the vestigial remembrance of Rabha traditional culture. Hence special emphasis was given in this collection trip for the collection of Rabha masks which have now become almost extinct.

Only the collection of ethnographic objects will not serve the purpose. Associated field data denoting their functional role in cultural environment are also essential. Without field data and museum exhibits, it may not be possible to acquaint the visitors with other cultural in the museum. Study and research with museum specimens may not be feasible without field data. It may also be difficult to write the cultural history with specimens which are not provided with field data of their own. Therefore, the maintenance of both the cultural artifacts and their associated field data is of paramount importance in the contemporary museological activities to make the museum structurally equipped and functionally potential.

From the functional point of view, both for imparting visual education and also for developing a museum for ethnographic study and research, both the cultural artifacts and their associated field data are essential prerequisite. To discharge this responsibility the museum maintains and preserves the cultural artifacts for the posterity and also maintains the field data in the museum so as to help the scholars in writing the culture history of a region or a community or a culture trait. The museum, therefore, occasionally brings out publication for maintaining the field data in published form to make them available conveniently to the scholars. For the purpose, instead of making analytical study, the ethnographic data are simply presented systematically in such publication, in the form of documentation without going for detailed analytical study. From this point of view, this publication of the Indian Museum has furnished the field data of the Jungle Rabha masks and masked dance in the form of documentation from the anthropological standpoint. These published data related to the museum specimens may be profitably utilised by the scholars in future for writing the culture history of the region.

References

Das, B. M. 1956, Physical Character of the Rabhas of Assam, Man in India, Vol. 36, No. 2, p. 92.

Das, B. M. 1960, Ethnic Affinities of the Rabhas, Guwahati.

Dalton, E. T., 1872, Descriptive Ethnology of Bengal, Government Printing Press, Calcutta.

Hunter, W. W. 1974, (Reprinted), A Statistical Account of Bengal, Vol. X, Delhi : D. K. Publishing House.

Das, A.K. and Raha, M.K. 1967, The Rabhas of West Bengal, Calcutta: Cultural Research Institute, Special Series No. 9.

Das, A.K. and Raha, M.K. 1966, Handbook on Scheduled Castes and Scheduled Tribes of West Bengal, Calcutta : Cultural Research Institute, Special Series No. 8.

Endle, Rev. S., 1911, The Kacharis, Macmillan & Co., London.

Friend-Pereira, G. E., 1912, The Rabhas in Census of Assam 1911, Vol. III, part- I, pp. 145.

Grierson, G. A. 1903, Linguistic Survey of India, Vol. III, part II, pp. 105, Calcutta.

Mitra, A., 1953, Census 1951 - West Bengal, The Tribes and Castes of West Bengal, Alipore, pp. 76.

Pal, Surajit K. 1992, Agrarian situation in a village of Buxa Forest Division, Jalpaiguri District of West Bengal, Journal of Indian Anthropological Society, Vol. 27, pp. 20-34. Calcutta.

Raha, M. K., 1989, Matriliny to Patriliny - A Study of the Rabha Society, New Delhi : Gian Publishing House.

Risley, H. H. 1891, The Tribes and Castes in Bengal, Bengal Secretariat Press, Calcutta.

Risley, H. H. 1905, The People of India, Bengal Secretariat Press, Calcutta.

Sanyal, C. 1965, The Rajbansis of North Bengal.

Sarkar, S. R. 1990, The Masks of West Bengal, Indian Museum, Kolkata.

Sarkar, S. R. 1992, "Bengal", in Saryu Doshi (ed) Tribal India - Ancestors, Gods and Spirits, Marg Publications, pp. 45-56, Bombay.

Sarkar, S. R. 2001, "Masks of West Bengal : An Anthropological Study", in S. C. Malik (ed), Rupa - Pratirupa - Mind Man and Mask, Indira Gandhi National Centre for the Arts, pp. 221-231, New Delhi.

Index